Delphire

I

The King Of Shadows

To my best friend:

who decided the door would be sexy,
now you finally get to see his full story.

I love you mate.

ACT ONE

Parc One

Introduction and the Beginning-The Outcast

I sat alone, up in the crow's nest of my ship, the Outcast, as my crew bustled below, doing their daily tasks. I had given my typical watchman, Crow, a break, or more accurately, I had wanted to be the first to see it. Besides, it was nice up here, the wind softly blowing through my green curls, and my tail swaying with the salty air.

Myself and my crew of mercenaries had been summoned for a proposal by a mage in Raenmora, a mountainous region near the coast. The mage had not given his reasoning for my summons, but he had requested me by name – not Blaidd

Delphire, as was the name I now went by, but my birth name, Romulus Neverglade, of which few knew. That itself was enough for me to drop everything and head straight to Daemons Keep, where the mage lived.

This mage was well known and, quite frankly, one of the most powerful mages – if not the most powerful – in the country. Mogotsi Nightshade, King of Shadows and the Keeper of Time. What the King of Shadows wanted with me, I did not know, and in a way, I was scared to know. Unfortunately, my curiosity outweighed my fear, as we had set sail the moment the crew had returned to the ship that night. That at least was not uncommon, working as a do-it-all crew of mercenaries and treasure hunters (no, we are not pirates – a cruel comparison). Apart from my first mate and best friend, Beckett, none of the crew members knew exactly where we were going, nor anything that had been in that letter. Not that it contained much anyway.

Dear Romulus Neverglade,

A development of much importance necessitates an audience with you at your earliest convenience. The purpose of this meeting would be to discuss your services. I trust you understand the gravity of this matter and will grant this request in due diligence.

Sincerely,

Mogotsi Nightshade

I wasn't sure if this guy knew being ominous would get me to come faster, but if it was, his plan worked. One thing that bothered me above the others was how he seemed to know my name. Yes, he was a powerful mage, so I'm sure he had his ways and methods of knowing what he wanted, but that didn't stop me from wanting to know what those ways and methods were.

It made Beckett nervous, and he didn't think it was a good idea to go. We – the crew of the Outcast – did have a not-so-great reputation. We were mercenaries, and when someone came to us with enough coin, we did what they wanted. Alongside the remedial tasks – scoping out an area, going to "fetch" things or information, and helping with territory disputes – there were the less favorable tasks. theft, kidnapping, and on rare occasions, paid assassinations. Unless the target was an unfavorable individual, however, I would deny the requests.

The crew of the Outcast were not the most favorable people, but we were far from monsters. In either direction, however, we had a lot of enemies, and the King of Shadows...well, I hoped we had never accidentally crossed him in some way, and this was just a ploy to get me to go to him so he could kill me – as Beckett had made it very clear he believed was the motive for my summons. That was why we had decided not to tell the crew where exactly we were going. I didn't want them to panic for no reason, in case Beckett was right. Besides, Mogotsi had requested me specifically, so me specifically he was going to see.

As I sat up in the crow's nest, along the seemingly never-ending expanse of the sea, a small shape began to form. Staggering dark stone cliffs glittered as the sun began to set behind them, just a barely visible shape from where we were now. The cliffs of Raenmora. "LAND AHEAD!" I called, then began to make my way down from the crow's nest, jumping most of the way, a rope in hand to catch my fall. Several of the crew members turned to face me as I landed on deck with a slight thump, my paws neatly catching me, claws slightly scratching the wood, where, as it were, was already scratched from my several landings.

"Captain," a male voice called. My ears perked to Beckett's voice. I turned to face him. Compared to my green hair, large wolf-like ears the size of a tuba, long thin furred tail capped with a plume of green fur the shape of a maple leaf – as well as my large pawed feet and round, amber eyes – Beckett looked extremely human. He was well-tanned and built, as every sailor should be, with sun-bleached brown hair that traced his strong features, the tone matching his brown almond-shaped eyes. He was your stereotypical human sailor. In due respect, he acted like it as well.

"Can I talk to you for a second?" He leaned slightly into me, his voice low as if he expected my ears to be on the side of my head like a normal person, and not on the top of my head as they were. Besides, thanks to giant ears and my magic, I could hear someone whisper from below deck in the middle of a storm while I was in the crow's nest. A blessing and a curse – as quite frankly, sometimes I don't want to hear what the crew members were saying in their sleep.

"Course," I grinned, tail swaying. Beckett placed his hand on my shoulder, ushering me away from the gaggle of the less-than-human crew and up to the bridge where only one other crew member stood at the wheel, Beckett's blonde-haired wife, Valarie. Val fit in a little better with the crew of misfits, at least by appearance –

compared to Beckett. She was human, but when she was younger, the girl was in a fire, burning half of her body, and of course, she still bore the scars from it.

-Intermission-

Ah yes, I should explain that quickly. The Outcast and her crew were formed of, well Outcasts. Those with less favorable reputations (but not criminals- well...) where abandoned or left home (as myself), and just those who needed somewhere who had nowhere. Over time the crew had become a family of misfits, and quite frankly, I wouldn't have it any other way.

The Crew is as follows:

Blaidd: That would be me- a Deformed wolf Anima-Spirit who ran away from a distant country at a young age, built the outcast, and now serves as captain.

Beckett: My first mate, a human whose mother left when he was a boy and a father died at sea.

Valerie: Beckett's wife, human. Mother died at birth, and her father stopped caring about her after her accident, so she ran away.

Crow: half-wood elf. He was an "accident" child and left home after substantial abuse.

Finley: Half mermaid half human. outcasted because neither humans nor merfolk would accept him as a "halfbreed."

Zeek: mouse anima spirit. He has a speech impairment so it was hard for him to find work.

Lulu: Bunny anima spirit. On the run after accidentally killing her brother in a burst of magic and her family hunting her down.

Culo: Drow. Outcasted from his homeland for reasons unknown.

Tricks: Faefolk. She left Faerie and needed a job.

Shade: Banshee. She's mute.

Daisy and Posey: Nymph twins. Their forest was invaded, and the two were only able to escape with a single flower from their lands keeping them alive via magic. They lashed back at the humans who destroyed their homes and are on the run.

Lion: Fire elf. Military deserter.

Little: Kelpie. After finding out how brutal his race was he left his homeland.

Pitch: Half orc half wood elf. He was born with facial deformities, and while he was accepted, he never felt like he belonged anywhere until finding the outcast.

Dapper: human. Outcasted after he lost half of his face.

Sketch: Malign (demon-type creature). Ex-assassin of whom, because of his previous life, wanted to leave his homeland, and originally was only taking passage on the Outcast, before deciding to join the crew.

Bugs: Spider Demon. He never gave a reason as to why he left his homeland but joined the crew after being unable to find somewhere that trusted him enough to hire him.

Ghost: I... don't know. Ghost is a tall white figure with yellow eyes and a wide mouth. He has no noticeable features - no nose, ears, etc, and he does not talk, although he seems to understand the common tongue. He just appeared on the ship one day. The crew all likes him.

Buck: Sun elf. Left home after his village began to find ways to torment or try to kill him as bad things happened around him, claiming him to be cursed.

Doe: Fae folk. Followed Buck.

Glorian: Moon elf. He was born to rich parents who didn't want him and typically neglected him entirely, so he ran away.

Now, if you didn't notice, all names listed above, except for Beckett and Valarie, are not real names. This is one of the things I make a point to mention before anyone joins my crew. One of the goals of the *Outcast* is to come somewhere where you can be yourself and leave your old life behind. We all come from less than favorable lives, and it's not something that, on the ship, I want to be forced out of any one of the crew members. Their pasts are something for them to say, and only if they want.

The nicknames are a way to help new crew members feel like part of the family and to help them feel free of the (painful for most of us) pasts that are left behind when someone joins the

Outcast. I have no rules about staying or leaving the crew. Members are free to come and go as they want, and if they do leave, they are always welcome back aboard.

There had only ever been one crew member to leave the *Outcast* so far, a faun by the name of Trog, who once he had enough saved, left the *Outcast* to build an inn. He had expressed multiple times how he missed the land and the forests, so while it was still sad when he left, no one was surprised.

That was the point of the *Outcast* after all. She was unmoored from flags and borders, a sanctuary for the world-weary who seek refuge beyond the fog. A silent vow holds her crew together: contribute whatever talents you possess. Here, lost souls can mend, acquire new skills, or simply be free from the world's harsh gaze. Laughter mingles with the salty air as shared meals and stories, illuminated by flickering lanterns, we hold a kinship stronger than blood.

For those severed from their roots, the *Outcast* becomes a chosen family. A sense of belonging, once a stranger, now resonates within the very timbers of the ship. We flourished on acceptance, a beacon to the spirit's yearning for connection in a tempestuous world. For some, the *Outcast* is a temporary haven, a place to heal and find their ground. For most, it becomes their permanent home, a vessel that carries them not only across the waves but away from the shadows of their past, toward a future embraced by the warmth of a new family.

Val looked over at the two of us, her brown eyes fixing on Beckett, who shook his head no. With that, Valarie adjusted her gaze, turning her focus back on the wheel.

"I know you didn't want to tell the crew where we were going, but as we get closer, they are getting more curious. Dapper and Sketch keep bugging me, and I've had nearly half of the rest of the crew asking what is going on. We have never not told them before. They know something is up, Blaidd." Beckett said, his brown eyes focused on mine, his thick brows furrowed.

My long tail swayed, my eyes wandering away from Beckett and to the deck where various crew members were working and talking to one another. I couldn't help but smile slightly as I saw

Ghost sitting with Daisy and Posey, who appeared to be trying to teach the creature how to play chess, then bursting into laughter as Ghost proceeded to eat the chess pieces. Little, who was watching from nearby, made his way over, trying to stop Ghost – his explanations getting him nowhere as the twins bent over with laughter.

"Mogotsi requested me," I looked back at Beckett. "In case this is something dangerous, I don't want to pull anyone else into it. Once I leave, you are welcome to tell the crew what is going on, but until I am off this ship, no one is to know anything beyond the fact that I am going to meet with someone. Understand?"

"You're going alone?" If possible, his brows furrowed more as he crossed his arms.

"I'll be fine, and if I'm not, then the rest of the crew will be. If anything happens, I want you to take charge, okay? Take care of them for me," I smiled toothily, bowing slightly, my tail swaying.

"Alright – but I would feel better if someone went with you," Beckett placed his hand on my head, playfully ruffling my hair.

"I'll be fine." I nudged his hand away, then patted the sword at my side, smiling at the brunette. Despite my being captain, Beckett was a few years older than me and had always reminded me of my brother back home, treating me like a little brother and taking care of me. Grace knows I need it as I tend to lose myself. His care did get irksome at times, as he would pester me about doing things that I seemed – in his eyes – too young to do. I was not old by any means – 18 years old and thriving, but I wasn't a baby either.

"I should be back on deck by tomorrow noon at the absolute latest. If I am not back by then, you don't need to wait for me," I smiled.

"No. I'm coming to get you if you're not back by then."

"Beckett."

"Romulus." He raised a brow, making sure I noticed his still crossed arms. I gasped when he spoke my real name – the last time anyone had called me that – apart from the letter was in fact, also Beckett – almost a year ago when I had first shown him the colorfully painted and patched together ship that was now the *Outcast*. He had thought I was joking about my plans for the ship, and he had scolded me about the reality of the idea. That's what he gets for relying on reality.

"Ship rules, Mr. Haddon!" I nearly yelled, catching myself before it came out too aggressive.

"Oh come on –"

"Your real name is Romulus?" An amused teenage voice spoke from behind Beckett and me. I snapped my head in the direction of the voice, my ears flattening. A small elvish boy with navy blue skin with white freckles that glittered across his skin, his silver eyes complimenting his white hair. Glorian. He leaned against the railing of the ship, doing nothing but eavesdropping. I stalked over to the boy, who shrank back ever so slightly, although I could tell he was trying to act brave.

"You speak a word to ANYONE about that piece of information, next time I throw you overboard, I will make sure that I throw you FROM the bow deck so you get bludgeoned by the keel and shredded by the barnacles that line this ship till your blood attracts the tuna fish and they rip what's left of you to shreds, eating you alive. While you go through this excruciating pain as you bleed out and suffocate, you will wish you were dead, and don't worry, you will die; because going through one of the worst and most painful ways to do so. Do you understand me, Glorian?"

"WOE-" Beckett placed his hand on my shoulder, tugging in an attempt to get me to back away from the elf, who looked as if he was about to start crying. My eyes stayed fixed on Glorian, waiting for a response. The boy nodded with a whimper. I took a few steps back, and he wasted no time getting around me and bolting to the main deck.

"Blaidd!" Beckett snapped, causing me to face him. "That was too far!"

"It wasn't like I yelled at him," I mused, my amusement not matched on Beckett's face.

"He's a kid!"

"He can handle it."

"He has been through enough." At Beckett's words, I went still, my ears lowering slightly. That was fair enough. I ran my hand through my curls. I didn't regret what I had said, although the longer Beckett glared at me, I began to.

"You're right – you're right, you're right –" I paced slightly, looking to the deck and to see if I could find the blue-skinned boy. It was easy enough to assume he had gone directly below deck where he could hide. I frowned, then looked to Beckett.

"You made your point though – I doubt he will even be able to utter it in his sleep."

"He better not. That name is my past. I want nothing to do with it anymore." I turned to face the sea. The sky was much darker now, the mountains covering what was left of the sun. The crew had begun to light the on-deck lanterns, which cast a warm glow over the ship and some areas of the waters below. My gaze turned to the cliffs ahead as Beckett walked to my side.

"That's why you want to go so badly – and why you don't want the crew to know what is going on...isn't it?" The sailor's gruff voice was a little softer than typical, causing me to turn my attention to him.

"Exactly. Somehow he knows my name, and I need to know why and how – and what he wants with me."

"Mogotsi is one of the most powerful mages in the country – if not the world. I'm sure knowing your name is nothing more than a simple little magic trick to him – Blaidd, he is probably only using it to draw you to him…you know that right?"

"Of course I do," my tail swayed, following the soft ocean wind. I kept my eyes on Beckett, a toothy grin spreading across my face. "And honestly, it just makes me all the more curious about why he wants to meet with me."

Part Two

The King of Shadows lives up to his name

After the *Outcast* was as close as I could get her to the cliffs without risking damage, I took a dinghy to the cliff edge, tying the boat to a rock. I managed to wedge the rope between a naturally formed hollow in the stone, securing the craft as best I could. While I was concerned about the tide and strong waves splintering the boat, I didn't have many other options. Thanks to the bright light of the two nearly full moons, I was able to see quite well, despite the full night that filled the sky. I made my way up the sea-dampened stones, climbing without incident until I reached the top. If there was one thing I was great at, after all, it was climbing.

When I reached the top, I had to pause to admire the sight before me. The castle was built into the side of the mountainous cliffs, and while it was striking from a distance, it was even more so up close. Beaten by the winds and spray of the sea, the base of the castle was coated in salt, making a fine transition from white to the black of the stone.

The castle itself looked nearly pieced together, as if over the centuries different rooms and towers had been added onto a much smaller castle. The different periods and architecture of each section were prevalent, but that didn't make the fortress any less beautifully striking. In fact, it added to the grandeur and awe of the thing. Vines and varying other foliage grew along the sides of the palace as if nature had begun to take over the building, getting lost in time.

Anyway, after taking in the view, I began to search for an entrance, which didn't take as long as I thought. There was a path only a mile windward of the fortress, with a stone path and staircase that led from a small row of docks straight from the sea to a back entrance of the castle. (I climbed those rocks for what I ask you? Your viewing pleasure, of course.)

I made my way to the doors, which were unexpectedly large, once dark stained – now weathered and pale – like the rest of the building. Steel ornaments bordered the frame of the door, swirling patterns laced with details of varying sizes and shapes of stars, all streaming and making their way to the handles of the double doors, which were in the shape of two crescent moons.

"Sexy," I murmured as I grabbed onto the smooth metal of the handles, my many rings making a soft clink sound as they made contact with the steel. My tail swayed – the metal was warmer than I had expected. The sun had set some time ago, and more than that, it had set leeward of the castle – on the other side. The metal should be far from pleasant to the touch by now. Even the metal of my rings, despite the warmth of my hands, where cold and bitter against my skin. I tried to ignore my fascination, however, and pulled open one of the doors.

Inside the fortress was kind of... for lack of a better word – underwhelming, at least compared to the exterior of the castle. Then again, this was just the back door – so to speak. The floors were made of dark wood, the walls the same stone as the exterior, although darker as they were less weathered. A large wrought iron chandelier hung from the ceiling unlit, the only source of light in the room the pale blue moonlight that shone through the tall fogged glass windows. The room was empty apart from that, just a basic back entrance to a palace fortress I suppose.

I began walking to the set of double doors on the other side of the room, stalking through the tall-ceilinged room, pushing them open, and immediately freezing. A very tall man, with gray skin and darker gray hair, with two large demon-like black horns – mismatched, one taller than the other, the curve of the horns narrowing in on each other – was standing only a few feet away. He looked as though he had been walking in the direction of the back hall, probably to investigate the sound of the doors opening. His sharp eyes focused on me, which in itself was horrifying. Where his eye whites should be, it was black, his irises white, as if his eyes were in reverse. Black markings surrounded his eyes, almost looking like eyeliner that, at the back corners of his eyes, went up in a thin sharp point, and in the front, down in a slight curve to his nose.

Two more markings trailed from under the center of his eyes that resembled black tears or a clown. He wore nothing beyond black trousers and a black cardigan, which showed his well-muscular chest and stomach. His large hands were tipped with long claw-like nails, a deep black starting at his fingertips and seeming to fade the further it went up his arm.

"You are very scary," was the first thing that came out of my mouth – not the best thing to say to someone that could snap your neck between their pinkies before you even knew what was happening, but hey. The man's expressionless face raised an eyebrow, which made me second-guess what I just said.

"I mean – scarily beautiful, and muscular – extremely..." I paused. "Do you work out your pinkies by any chance?"

"My...pinkies?" His voice was the deepest and sexiest monotone I had ever heard, especially for someone talking about their pinkies. There was no emotion in it whatsoever, which made his voice equal to being smoother than polished marble floors. If I wasn't on the verge of peeing myself before, I was now. I felt my face go warm, my vision blurring as my eyes widened for a long moment, my unfocused gaze set on his strong chiseled jawline.

"You are Romulus Neverglade, are you not?" His voice broke my space-out stare, causing me to blink and snap back into reality. My ears perked up as I stared up at the giant of a man, and I nodded.

"Yes – I am, but I go by Blaidd Delphire now." My brows furrowed slightly as I forced a smile.

"Of that, I am aware." He spoke, then after a moment's pause, tilted his head at me. As we made eye contact for some time, and I got the feeling I knew exactly who this was, it had not been what I was expecting. But then again, what can you expect from a king of shadows? I held my smile, tail flicking in impatience behind me. I was waiting for him to say something, but after a minute of silence, I was growing impatient. Then suddenly an odd feeling of curiosity washed around me. It was not me, although there were many things I was curious about, but this felt different. This was not my curiosity, this was not my emotion I was feeling. It was his.

As the king of shadows continued to keep his eyes on me, I felt his curiosity growing. Such an odd sensation, to not see an expression, but rather to feel it around you. Instead of asking what he was doing, or who he was, or what he wanted, I made sure my eyes were focused on his, then spoke, "What do you want to know?" The feeling of curiosity, while not fading, was suddenly mixed with amusement, and what felt like appreciation.

He nodded, straightening himself. "Follow me, Romulus Neverglade." With that, the King of Shadows turned and began to walk further into the palace.

"Blaidd." I chided but followed nonetheless. The inside of the palace, unlike the entrance room, was breathtaking. A wrought iron chandelier, alight with a white flame, hung high on the tall black wooden beamed ceiling.

The stone walls to my right were covered in tall stained glass windows that seemed to depict various images that represented each of the different elements (that being Time, reality, mind, light, dark, fire, water, earth, air, and ice) and an additional window, full of shapes and colors, although I couldn't imagine what it was to represent if anything at all. I decided I liked it.

To my left was a series of large open doors, each room different from the last, all seeming to surround themselves with various purposes and hobbies. There were two rooms, whose doors were larger than the rest, one a grand library, bigger than one I had ever seen, and the other appearing to be nothing more than an open sitting area with plush couches and a low table and fireplace.

There were various movements in each of the rooms, fae and elves, humans, and several other creatures busied themselves around the palace, some seeming to do various tasks, the others just walking in conversation or otherwise simply roaming the halls. I couldn't help but think it was strange how it was so busy inside, while it was still night outside, but I decided not to question it for the time being. My ears moved constantly with the sounds that seemed to come in all directions, not knowing where to focus themselves. At least the king of shadows did not live alone.

At one point, I had stopped, peeking in a room that appeared to be some type of music room. Various instruments filled the room in various sizes and colors. Nymphs played the piano while a goblin batted at a tambourine, a fawn singing along. Mogotsi had stopped when I did, and I only turned when I swore I could feel him smiling, only to be met by his expressionless face again.

Room after room and stained glass window after stained glass window we walked, until eventually reached a large double door at the end of the hall, only for the open doors to reveal another set of doors and another hall. This time, however, Mogotsi turned into the first door, and I was impressed to see he did not have to duck to get inside. As I followed, I was surprised to see this doorway led to a set of spiral stairs that led upwards. In silence I followed, still having no idea why I was here, to begin with.

Finally, we reached the top of the stairs, which appeared to be an office of some type. A row of full bookshelves sat against the wall, shaped around an arched window. A large dark wooden desk sat here on the back wall, empty and clean apart from an oil lamp and a closed book. The other walls were covered in shelves full of various magical and non-magical items, scrolls, and stacks of paper, with bottles of varying colored ink sitting along a row of floating crystals and a line of ten clocks, all varying in detail, shape, and color. There seemed to be space for two more on the display, but there were no more clocks to be found. The other wall of shelves was much the same, full of orderly-placed magical items and trinkets. If I wasn't so scared of this guy, I would be tempted to grab something just to see what it was.

Mogotsi made his way around the desk, where he finally sat down, then motioned for me to do the same in a wooden chair I swear had not been there a moment ago. Again, silence. This time, I decided to speak. "So you are the King of Shadows, Mogotsi Nightshade?" I kept my eyes trained on him.

"I am," he nodded. "I must admit, however, I do rather dislike that title. I am no king: I bear no crown. Nor do I make deals with the shadows. That is not my place nor my role." He kept his creepy white eyes on me as he spoke, and quite frankly, it was hard to look away. They were so white... I couldn't tell if his irises were glowing, or if it was simply the stark contrast of the black of his eye whites that made it appear as such. I nodded at his words. While he may not be a king of shadows, I understood just by looking at the guy where the name had come from. I mean – he may not have been a king, but he did live in a palace, and clearly had a large court of people who followed him, going off of those I had seen on our way up to the study.

"I've heard about you," I started after I was sure he was done speaking – I didn't want to be the person to interrupt the not-king of shadows. "You were the one who banished the great evil. Carnage – the prince of Shadows. It was your success that gave you the title, Mogotsi Nightshade, the king of shadows, and the keeper of time." I explained, my gaze still on him. That was the story I had heard since moving to this country. "Is it all true?" I asked.

"It is," there seemed to be a sadness in his air as he spoke, an odd feeling that sent chills down my spine. I had a feeling no matter what frame of time I worked for this guy, I would never get used to feeling his emotions. On the plus side, it made it easy to understand this was a conversation he was not really comfortable with or wanting to talk about.

After another long moment of silence, the forced smile I typically held fell yet again, one of my massive ears falling to the side, my earrings making a soft jingling sound. "Why am I here? – how do you know my name? What – what do you want with me?" I finally broke, unable to keep myself from speaking.

An air of amusement replaced the weird sad feeling as Mogotsi kept his gaze on me, and with that, he stood up. Unsure what to do, I stayed put in my chair. I watched as the large man looked to the bookshelf behind him, grabbing a book near to where he stood. "As mentioned in my letter to you, I require your services, and I am willing to pay you handsomely, with the potential of future...arrangements" He spoke as he pulled the book he must have been looking for, a red leather book with gold detailing and a cover that I couldn't quite read from where I sat. My tail twitched with interest – and the need to move. Gosh sitting still was so hard.

I did my best to stay attentive as he sat back down and began to flip through the book. "I'll do it," I kept my eyes on him. The white-eyed man lifted his eyes back to me, and I'm guessing if he had expressions, it would be one of those condescending faces moms make when you ask for a new toy at the store when you already know it's a no.

"I did not tell you what I needed as far as service?" It didn't sound like a question, but going off the lack of tone in his voice, I had a feeling it was probably ending with a question mark.

"You said and I quote 'pay you Handsomely' That's enough for me." I kept my eyes on him, as he stood stone still, looking at me. I simply shrugged. "But I need to know how you know my name."

"You display a boldness I was not expecting."

"And you do the opposite of speaking clearly and concisely." After I closed my mouth, I got a feeling I had gone too far, as Mogotsi stared at me for a long moment. I couldn't tell what he was feeling, or maybe he didn't know what he was feeling. This staring match went on for some time, and I was starting to feel like I needed to grab my sword when a wash of strong curiosity spread around me. Of all things after that – he was curious?

I let my mouth fall into its resting toothy smile. "So. I know you're this powerful mage – but I have gone to pretty great lengths to shield my identity. How do you know who I am?"

"What are you shielding your identity from? Your family lives in distant lands, they do not search for you. You have no ties, and no history in Eritis. If you can answer this, I can answer your question equally. Why do you fear who you are, Romulus Neverglade?"

With that, I clenched my jaw, pushing myself to my feet, my claws digging into the wooden floors, seething with anger. "I DON'T FEAR WHO I AM!" I bellowed, ears flat against my head and tail low with aggression.

"I cannot help but wonder if your outward expression fully reflects your internal sentiment." He didn't move, simply staying in his seat, his eyes on me. Even sitting down, the mage was near to my height as I stood standing. I leaned forward, pulling a knife from my belt, stabbing it into the desk only a few inches from Mogotsi's hand, my eyes focused on his as my shoulders rose and fell intensely with my breath.

"You know nothing." I growled, yanking my knife after a moment, the action tearing the wood in his desk. I shoved it back into its sheath and began stalking out of the room. I only made it to the door, however, my hand just reaching for the handle when Mogotsi spoke again.

"I know more than you believe I do, Romulus Neverglade. I be-"

"STOP SAYING THAT NAME!" I interrupted before the mage was able to finish his sentence, another potentially stupid move. I shrank back the second he stood up – I couldn't read what he was feeling, and that in itself was doing more than freaking me out. I eyed him, my hand on the handle of my sword. Beyond standing, he made no move. It felt like an eternity the two of us stood still –

before I realized, in a way, it had. As my eyes focused on Mogotsi, I made out a glow that had not been there before – or, a brighter glow, from his irises. He was using magic. My heart began to beat faster, as I came to the realization I could not move my body. While I was still breathing, the rest of me was stuck in time, proven as I tried to pull my sword from its sheath to no avail.

Mogotsi's head tilted ever so slightly as he accurately read the fear in my eyes, and after a long moment, his eyes ceased to glow, and I all but collapsed onto the floor. Now that I was free of the sensation, I wasn't sure if I had been breathing during that minute of stillness. I began to gasp, clutching my chest, pleading with my body to make up for the last minute it had been unable to breathe. My limbs also felt incredibly sore, as if everything in my body had stopped working for that minute, and now was working double-time to make it up.

"You should not let your emotions take over like that." The mage sat back down, his eyes never leaving me. I continued to hold my chest, fighting the urge to cry as my body struggled to adjust itself. My eyes trailed up to him, just barely able to make contact to where he sat.

"G-guardian of time, huh?" I clenched my jaw as I spoke, the simple action hurting more than I was expecting. Mogotsi nodded. I didn't know how to feel, if I should accept his proposal, listen to what he needed to retrieve – or leave now before he did something like that again. Something inside of me, however, told me that he would not do this again, not unless I needed it. Pausing my body was a warning, not anything more or anything less.

After a moment, I forced myself up, practically falling back into the chair. "Alright –" I started, "so about my services?" I felt a slight wash of interest and contentment come from the mage, who nodded. So he still intended to hire me. I could still feel that curiosity from Mogotsi, and that made me curious about what he was curious about – me right? But what about me was he curious about? Just me in general? I mean, I am myself, so I do understand that thought process; or was there more to that curiosity?

"You still desire to work for me?" Mogotsi would've sounded surprised, I'm sure, if he was capable. I forced my typical smile. "If you'll still take me. See despite your evident lack of care for me as a person –" I narrowed my round eyes slightly, "You said pay handsomely, and quite frankly myself and my crew could use the funds..." I paused for a moment. "What... do you consider paid handsomely?"

When he told me the amount, I almost peed myself again.

"That should be fine."

It took a good portion of time to go over the rest of our agreement, Mogotsi eventually walking me out just before sunrise. It shook me slightly how he seemed to all but pretend his whole – freezing my body in time – thing had never happened, and after my body had gone back to normal, it really did feel like nothing had happened. It was a warning, and I knew that much. The king of shadows was not a cruel person, despite what his title suggested. He had gotten the title defeating evil, not doing evil. Something in me trusted him and wanted to work and befriend this guy despite all.

Part Three

The resident moon-elf asks for a good hard smack in the face.

I wanted to go to my cabin and sleep the second I made it aboard the outcast, but I didn't get the chance as I was immediately swarmed with crew members asking what had happened, who I had met, and what our heading was. I regretted not telling them beforehand, although by the way Sketch and Culo looked at me, those two at least had figured it out.

"Are you ok Blaidd? you were gone all night!" Lulu's purple eyes looked teary, as if she had been crying, and was about to do so again. I playfully ruffled her white hair with a quick

"I'm alright"

"Do we have a heading?" Crow asked, his brows furrowed. He looked as if he had just woken up, his eyes groggy and long dark braid a mess.

"Yes- and no" I replied

"Who did you meet with Cap?"Little's green eyes were focused on me, his voice a little louder than the rest, even as more questions were belted at me-

"Did you sleep there?"

"Were you hurt?"

"Did we get a job?"

"What is the job?"

"Glorian jumped ship again." It was Lion who spoke that time, the muscular fire elf's arms crossed as he gazed at me, his gray eyes focused. With that, the rest of the crew went silent. In a moment my exhaustion was replaced with anger, my eye twitching, a smile still on my face.

"And no one went to go get him?!" I fought the urge to scream, and of course no one replied "Everyone back to your posts!" I growled, "Lion, not you- you tell me what happened?! And where is Beck!?" I watched as the rest of the crew shimmied to their posts, "Get her ready to go! I want to be on our way when I get back" That time I did scream at the crew, a mixture of anger and authority in my tone.

"I'm not entirely sure, he was gone when I went to wake up the crew this morning." Lion spoke as he pulled his ginger mane (heh) of hair back into a ponytail.

"And you were on watch?" I questioned. At that, the elves' long ears went down slightly.

"Yes captain." was all he said, his ex-military physique showing for a moment. I simply nodded.

"Remind me not to buy you a drink next time we go out together" My ear twitched, lips in a slight frown. He nodded.

"And you are triple sure he is not just hiding on the ship somewhere?"

"Yes captain." he nodded again and I let a sigh escape my lips.

"Alright-" I nodded, turning to lower the dingy again. I paused, glancing over at Lion as he moved to help me. "And Beckett?"

"Still sleeping, he was up late waiting for you. Only went to lay down when Val threatened him about two hours ago." I nodded at the gingers words, a wash of guilt and slight comfort knowing he had been waiting for me. "Are you sure you want to go alone to get Glorian?" Lion's words interrupted my thoughts.

"Yeah, it won't take long. No point in dragging anyone else out." I frowned. Lion's stern face nodded, and while I got the feeling that had been his way of offering to come with, I saw no point. "I want you here. You know how everything works around the ship, do your duties, and make sure everything is ready when I get back." I smiled encouragingly at the elf, who nodded.

I began searching immediately when I made it to land, and while part of me thought he could have gone into the palace and was hiding in one of the rooms in Mogotsi's palace, I knew that wasn't in his character. More likely than not Glorian had gone around the palace and into the mountains that surrounded it, wanting to get as far away from the sea and the Outcast as possible. This wasn't the boy's first time jumping ship, and by this point, he had an M.O. to follow. Every time he would not take anything with him- not that he had any personal effects on him anyway- and ran as fast and as far as he could, till he found somewhere to hide. There he would stay for an hour or so, before running again. Every time he did this I found him, and while he may not have known it, I knew deep down Glorian knew I was going to find him, and strangely liked the affirmation of knowing I would look for him and get him every time. I knew I likely would do the same thing if I were in his situation.

Glorian was not like the rest of the crew members, in that his coming to the crew was different. It hadn't been as simple as the rest of the crew, and the elf made that known by his constant jumping ship at any chance he got. The problem was that he was good on a ship, and not only knew his way around and how to complete all the tasks he was given but also enjoyed working on the Outcast. I understood why he left, but given the fact that he did enjoy his life, I didn't understand it.

I searched around the palace, and areas around till I was sure the boy had made it past the palace grounds, when I had to begin making my way into the mountain paths. Knowing Glorian, he would keep to the paths as they were the safest option, and as he was running, and had no way of helping if he did get hurt, he would choose the safest option, no matter how likely it would be that he was found doing so.

I found Glorian faster than I had been expecting, which was a pleasant turn of events. The small blue-skinned elf was sitting against a pine tree, hugging his arms as he sat in the cold mountain air. He looked up when he heard me approaching, quickly looking away, pulling his knees to his chest. I sat down beside him, waiting a long moment for him to speak the first word, which, after a few minutes, he did.

"Blaidd-" he still kept his silver eyes off me, and so, I did the same, the two of us sitting side by side, our eyes focused off to the view in front of us. Glorian had found a good spot to rest. The tree we sat against was the only one in our direction over a section of hanging rock, so it was a clear view of the mountains and forests that seemed to stretch for miles beyond us.

"Here to drag me back?" He grumbled, making a small movement so his chin rested on his arms. I sighed, tilting my head, still not looking at the elf.

"I don't know, you found a pretty good view here; I may just stay here for a while and listen to the trees."

"Listen to the trees?" He finally turned to face me, his nose wrinkled in a snarky kind of amusement.

"Oh yes, they have a lot to say." I looked back at him, a small smile on my lips. "Besides it would be quite rude to not listen to them when all they want is someone to care." I closed my eyes, a soft, cool breeze blowing through my curls. Glorian stayed quiet for some time, causing me to open my eyes after a moment or so of silence. He looked confused, his eyes back out in the direction of the view in front of where we sat. "Do you ever take time to listen to the trees?" I smiled at the boy, who looked back at me, his brows still furrowed in confusion.

"I don't think I can hear them." He frowned, "what kind of stuff do they talk about?"

"Oh all kinds of stuff, but they really like to tell stories." I smiled, looking up into the branches of the pine where we sat, my tail resting itself across my legs.

"What is this one saying?" Glorian followed my gaze, his expression softening. I stayed silent for some time, listening as the old pine told his tale. Eventually, as he continued, I closed my eyes, listening to the words he spoke, envisioning those of whom he spoke, and the tale played out in my mind. After he was done I opened my eyes and nodded, thanking the old tree for sharing his story with me, then looked back at Glorian, and repeated the words he had told me.

"Centuries etched in bark, I, the ancient pine, have stood. My roots, gnarled fingers, grasp the earth's beating heart. I watched the world grow. Then, a whisper on the wind, a flicker of light – a child, hair the color of spun moonlight, with eyes that mirrored a winter's day. Every dawn, she'd dance beneath my emerald embrace, her laughter a melody spun from leaves. One day, a new melody joined the chorus. A young man, his hair kissed by the sun, his eyes holding the promise of a coming sunrise. Beneath my canopy woven of starlight, they'd weave tales of their own. Timid touches, elegant dances, whispered secrets, a love blooming like a wild rose unfurling its heart. An unknown warmth, a current in the ancient flow of my sap, stirred within me. I, the silent observer, became the keeper of their story. The mountains stood sentinel, the wind their confidante, and beneath my timeless boughs, their love story, a brushstroke on the canvas of eternity, became forever intertwined with mine."

As I repeated his words, I hadn't thought when my gaze shifted from Glorian and back to the view beyond me, yet again enveloping myself in the tale. When I was done, both the elf and I sat in silence for a long while, till Glorian eventually broke the silence.

"No way," he spoke quietly as if he was still trapped in the tale, as I had been a moment before he spoke. "There's no way that's what the tree said! You're making that up! "he scoffed, then paused. "... aren't you?"

I simply smiled at Glorian, who narrowed his eyes, still looking back at me, "aren't you..." he repeated as if making sure I had heard.

"Why would I lie about that?" I raised an eyebrow "down right disrespectful to the tree." I shook my head in disappointment. Glorian sat staring at me in silence, still contemplating what I had said, before frowning.

"Trees don't talk. You're crazy." He rolled his eyes, then looked back at the view. I leaned slightly, digging in my small leather hip bag at my side, pulling out a small bottle of amber liquid, and downing a good portion of it before lowering it from my lips.

"Dont tell that to the ents-" I spoke rhythmically, staring out at the landscape before holding the bottle out to the moon elf beside me. He stared at it for a long while, not making a move to take the bottle, causing me eventually to look back over at him.

"Rude." I chided.

"I'm underage." Glorian scoffed, his eyes surveying me as if I had committed some type of unspeakable evil.

"And do I look like your mother, Glorian?" I raised an eyebrow, tilting the bottle encouragingly

"You actually kind of do, to be honest." his brows furrowed in a sudden switch to seriousness, which caused my eyebrows to go up.

"I ... .don't know how I feel about that-" I frowned, staring somewhat blankly at him.

"I think it's your hair- to be honest." he eyed my long green curls. I nodded in response, then shook my head

"That's not the point!" I quacked, shaking my head. "You live on my ships you take the sips, come on, you know you want some!" I encouraged again, shaking the bottle again tauntingly.

"I don't want to be on your ship- if you remember why we are sitting here right now!? Glorian snapped, gently pushing the bottle away and turning his head in the opposite direction of where I sat. I frowned my ears going back.

"More apple juice for me then." I shrugged and went to put the bottle to my lips when the elf's hand grabbed onto it, his eyes focused intensely on mine.

"Apple juice?"

"Yep." I nodded, and in an instant he snatched the bottle away, smelling it to see if I was telling the truth.

"Oh my gosh." he looked back at me, "It is apple juice."

"I told you." I scoffed, crossing my arms " I may be a captain and be known to be reckless, but I don't need alcohol on me all the time my goodness Glorian! Do I look like a pirate?"

We made eye contact for an uncomfortable amount of time, Glorian's brows furrowed and he started to open his mouth, but I spoke first.

"Sailing. Mercenaries." I narrowed my eyes, causing the boy to close his mouth. After another long moment, I jumped to my paws, tail swaying as I stretched my arms above my head.

"Ok, I'm bored now, time to go home." I kept my hands behind my head as I started walking, but only after taking a few steps my ears shifted back at the realization Glorian had not made a move to stand up, much less follow me. I turned back around, facing him.

"Come on." I did my best not to sound pushy, crouching down and holding out my hand, my head tilting and ear flopping to the side. "The rest of the crew is waiting for us."I smiled encouragingly.

Glorian didn't look at me, his eyes downcast to the bottle in his hands, turning over and swirling the amber liquid inside. "Why did my parents never come looking for me-" he finally spoke, his voice broken as if he was trying not to cry.

"Glorian-" the second the boy had spoken a wash of emotion waved over me, a feeling of guilt and regret knowing what the boy had been through. I crouched lower, till I was right in front of him, my eyes just a bit higher than his own.

"I know they never cared about me- that's why I left- but... but I thought my leaving was what would make them...love me-" He lifted his head, his silver eyes welling with tears, although he was forcing them back, making sure the liquid did not touch his cheeks.

"Especially after you kidnapped me- my ransom was public- why- why did they never-" His words broke, and before I knew what was happening he latched onto me, arms around my neck in a hug. I didn't know how to react, or what to do for a long moment, and simply hugged the boy back, awkwardly wrapping my arms around him, and lifting the small moon-elf up.

It was weird to think this now sobbing boy was somehow only a year younger than me technically speaking, and not just because I was taller than the average anima-spirit. He felt so small and frail, although truthfully, that was how most of the crew on the outcast truly was. A group of people who had been through some of the worst things imaginable, all forced together on a ship of whose name bore exactly what we were. Outcast.

"Please take me home-" Glorians voice was hard to understand between his tears and how it was muffled, as his head was pressed against my shoulder, although I knew what he meant. He didn't mean back to his parents who had abandoned him, or Tarrin, the city he had been raised in, but his home now, on the outcast. I nodded, sighing deeply.

"I am kid, I am..." My words trailed off as I thought about how he had come to join the crew in the first place. How I had tricked him onto the ship the day he had run away, and held him for ransom. One thing I had never told Glorian, was how I had gotten into contact with the boy's parents only two days after he had been taken. How they had told me to keep him or sell him off as a slave somewhere. Even when I had lowered the Ransome considerably, knowing they would well be able to afford their son's safe return home. While the circumstances were considerably different, it did remind me of my parentage, and as I continued to carry Glorian back to the ship, Mogotsi's words rang in my ears. No, my family hadn't come to look for me either.

Part Four

A break in the wind

After we got back to the *Outcast*, I let Glorian have the rest of the day to himself. There was enough crew to cover the lad, and he clearly had a lot on his mind. I may be a captain, but I am no taskmaster after all. The ship was ready to go by the time we had gotten back, as I had instructed the crew, and while I had hoped Beckett and all would be awake, I had to map out where we were going on my own. We had our heading, a town only a few days' journey east of Mogotsi's palace and Raenmora, a large island off the coast of Ethenal, known as the Isle of Whitview.

It was a clear day with smooth waters, so there was no need for the extra help. By noon, most of the crew was sitting on deck, talking, eating, or partaking in other various tasks. I stood behind the wheel, letting my mind wander as I kept the ship steady. I still had questions about Mogotsi, and could tell there was more to his story than was known. Something inside me knew our interactions would not end simply when I got this crystal for the guy.

A Harbinger stone. That was what the king of shadows had hired me to obtain. I didn't know much about the glorified rocks, apart from what I had heard several years ago from a merchant sailor I had only met in passing. The stones were extremely rare and not completely natural in their making. Not something that could be casually dug up. The Harbinger Stones were made when a diamond was formed under a fae burial on a Kelsier moon (when both moons rested on the same phase – yet another rare occurrence that only happened every seven years, sort of like an eclipse, but cooler). When starlight fell onto the burial, it enchanted the diamond, causing it to have the ability to hold any enchantment the wielder desired, as long as they were pure of heart, of course. It was said the enchantment could be manipulated and changed if the stone changed hands, but when one individual enchanted the stone, the enchantment would never change for that person. A one-and-done deal per person.

It was commonly understood that the creation of the Harbinger stones was a blessing from Grace directly (one of the creation deities) as their creation directly involved the Kelsier moons, and how Grace had always been directly tied to the moons. Needless to say, the stones were rare, and there were only a few even known to exist. I couldn't help but wonder what Mogotsi would use the stone for when he got it. The stone would be nothing more than a pretty rock if he was not pure of heart, and while I wasn't sure what exactly makes someone pure of heart, I had my doubts about the guy. Maybe it was just his face, or maybe

I was overthinking... I mean, he was the one who had banished Carnage, so maybe it was just his face. While it was hard not to wonder, really, it wasn't my place. He had hired me to get the stone, not to know what he was doing with it.

I yawned, resting my head on the wheel as I let my thoughts fade, well, as much as I was capable. I was still exhausted and could fall asleep standing up if I let myself at this point. While it had only been a few hours since leaving the castle, I hadn't gotten a wink of sleep, forcing myself up until Beck decided to get up. I wanted to talk to him, to let him know what had happened before I rested. Besides, it wasn't that I didn't trust my crew, in fact, quite the opposite, but I still liked either Beckett or myself to be on deck during the day. At night, I could care less, although thanks to my constant inability to fall asleep at night, I usually was on deck till at least three, then back before the sun was fully risen unless I had business in my cabin, which given the nature of the *Outcast* and the "job" of its crew, was not often granted the fact that as long as the skies weren't crying down, I would bring my business on deck with me.

"Captain?" Crow's voice practically made me jump out of my skin – as someone who hears everything, the fact that I had not heard his footsteps was more than unnerving – had I actually fallen asleep there for a minute? I turned to face the boy, his brown eyes focused on me, a slight look of amusement in his eyes.

"Sorry –" he spoke quietly.

"Don't apologize," I shook my head, chuckling slightly myself. "Also, come on, I thought you would know by now to just call me Blaidd." I straightened myself, stretching my arms for a moment.

"Right." The boy smiled, then his lips fell into a frown again. "Do you want me to take the wheel? You look a little... you know."

"How long did I sleep for?" I couldn't help but laugh, knowing that I had likely in fact fallen asleep. Crow looked down, then back up at me, his hand rubbing his neck.

"Not too long, I think. I don't know. I just looked over and you were out." he smiled with amusement, then made a move to slide in front of me, his hands grabbing onto the wheel. I didn't fight him, letting go and taking a step back, my tail swaying ever so slightly.

"...that's unfortunate." I frowned, looking up at the sky to make sure we hadn't stayed too far off course.

"You should sleep." The boy smiled slightly, although his words were genuine and a little too serious for my liking. I knew he was right, but the idea made me uncomfortable. The fact that Crow had said it also made me want to do it less. I grumbled inaudible words, looking down at my paws. Crow sighed.

"I'll come wake you when Beck is up if you want?" He offered, and at that, I nodded; too exhausted to think of a good comeback. Crow kept his eyes forward for a while, his eyes traveling to the small table beside the wheel where a map and compass sat, a flat-bottomed stone sitting on top of Whitview – what I used as my heading marker. After a long moment of silence, and my brain too melted to even move, Crow looked back at me.

"Pardon my asking – but why do you hate sleeping so much, Blaidd?"

"I don't hate it," I yawned, "It hates me." I rubbed my hand over my face, trying to brush some of my hair out of my face, a failed attempt as the same chunk of hair that always fell in my face fell back into place.

Crow kept his eyes on me for a long while before speaking, as if he was trying to figure out what exactly I had meant. "I'm sorry," he finally spoke, his words quiet, more of a mumble. "Get some sleep, Blaidd." Crow smiled softly. When he was done speaking, I nodded, and with that, made my way down to my cabin, and the second my head hit the pillow, I was asleep. I slept way longer than I should have, but still not quite as long as I could have. If Crow hadn't kept his deal with me – albeit waiting three hours after Beckett was up to get me – I could have slept for a week straight. In total, I slept around six hours give or take, and even after I was awake, I wasn't really awake.

I was thankful that Beckett decided not to talk to me right away, as I made my way to the wheel and stood silently, watching as Valarie stood at her typical place at the wheel, Beckett by her side. My first mate turned his attention to me as he saw me climbing the stairs, smiling encouragingly. Beckett was one of the few people who understood how the first twenty minutes after I was awake, I was still asleep, and unless it was urgent – where my brain would finally switch on – it was better to not talk to me, as any of the information retained after my waking was passed through my brain like it had never been there to begin with.

I sat down on the deck, leaning my head against the blue-painted wooden railing, sitting in the closest I could get my abnormally long shins to a crisscross, my hands on my thighs. I half watched as Beckett kissed his wife on the forehead, before muttering an "I love you" to her, and walking over, sitting down beside me. My head immediately flopped onto my friend's shoulder as I stared blankly at the wooden flooring for at least ten minutes. I probably could have fallen asleep there and then if I wanted, but I resisted. Plus, something was off. No, not necessarily off, different.

"She sounds different –" I tried to speak, my words coming out half-mumble.

"What?" Beck turned his head slightly.

"Valerie." I lifted my head, looking at him. "She sounds different."

Beckett narrowed his eyes, his thick brows furrowing. "In what way?"

"I don't know... she's just... different," I yawned, my ears tilting back as I did so. I placed my head back on the brunette's shoulder. Beckett's gaze had traveled from me to Valarie, his eyes focused on his wife.

"It doesn't sound bad –" I tilted my head back, looking at Beckett. "Just different."

I knew Beckett wasn't one to throw away what I said, no matter how strange or random it may seem. The two of us had been friends for years, and while it took the human a while to get used to me, he eventually came to understand that I wasn't completely crazy.

"Let me know if anything changes –" he frowned, his eyes going back to me. I lifted my head again, nodding. We sat in silence for a while, Beckett's eyes on his wife and mine down to the deck and the crew.

Eventually, Beckett looked back at me, his eyes focused on mine as he made eye contact. "So" he started, "how'd it go?"

With those words, I immediately flew into a tangent, finally awake and ready to tell my first mate everything that had happened. He listened intently as I relayed everything from the castle's interior, to Mogotsi, then to our conversation, his magic, the people in the palace, and how I had been able to scope out the area slightly when looking for Glorian. I could tell almost immediately after explaining how the King of Shadows had trapped me in time, that Beckett did not like this deal, and definitely didn't trust him.

"It was a test, I could tell, just a warning –
or reminder, of who he is."

"That, Blaidd, was a threat. He was
threatening you." By this point in our conversation,
the brunette seemed to be getting generally
frustrated. While I understood his point of view, I
also didn't understand why he was getting so
frustrated. I hadn't suffered any real harm.

"I don't think it was. You didn't meet him
Beck, you didn't... feel him the way I did."

"First off, don't ever use that phrasing
again. Second, I don't care. You said it hurt. He was
hurting you." His hands moved, his frustration as
his brown eyes widened, trained on me.

We stared at one another for a long time,
and while there were many things I wanted to say, I
made sure to choose my words carefully for when I
finally spoke, a sigh escaping my lips before I did
so. "When a child goes to steal, you gently slap

their hand." My left ear twitched. "When someone pulls a sword on you, you move to defend yourself."

Another long pause.

Beckett sighed, running his hand through his hair, pushing it with the wind. "Alright." he shook his head, eyes lifting back to me. "I don't like it, but I'm not your boss." he gently punched me in the shoulder. I was unable to stop the smile from spreading across my lips. A genuine smile, not the fake toothy thing I typically held.

"So..." he started again, his eyes casting to Val, who was still at the wheel, then back to me. "A Harbinger stone?

ACT TWO

Part Five

How the heck did he get my diary?

The *Outcast* made the sight of land three days later, and Crow's call was a lot of weight off my shoulders. This was not going to be a quick venture by any means, so the faster we made progress, the happier I was.

From what Mogotsi had told me, there was a map to the current known location of the stone, but that map had been traded, inherited, given away, and eventually sold to a merchant on the Isle of Whitview. How he knew all of this, I don't know, although I got the feeling it fell into the same category as how he knew my name – and being the whole keeper of time thing. I still had a lot of questions about that whole title.

Another thing that struck me as more than odd was how he knew the stone's history and the history of the map itself and did not simply come to retrieve the stone himself. The Harbinger stone was legendary, surely it was important enough for him to retrieve himself? With his height, big muscles, and moderately scary face, Mogotsi would likely be able to do this a lot quicker than myself. Nonetheless, I was happy with the promised funds and the prospect of more jobs. While we certainly were not poor on the *Outcast*, we were not rich by any means, so having something extra and consistent would be good for both the ship and her crew.

As we approached the isles, I was taken aback at how green they were. I had not been to Whitview in some years, and the last I had been, it was more settled. It seemed in the years since nature had retaken the isles, and while there was still a visible port and buildings along the coastline, it was mostly covered in a thick forest that seemed to cover the whole of the isles, from island to island. One thing that was fascinating about the isles was the large stone bridges that led from island to island – any land big enough to walk on, there was a bridge. One of these bridges led from the port island to the largest island, where I needed to go.

After making port and giving a briefing to my crew – as if had been agreed to the fact that they could wander the isles in shifts, so long as there was one or two of them on the *Outcast* at a time – and agreeing for all to be back on the ship by the time I got back, I gave myself twelve hours just in case finding the merchant and getting a hold of the map proved to be difficult.

While I had intended to go myself, Beckett, Valarie, and Glorian (shocking, right?) had volunteered to go with me. I needed to convince Beck and Val to take the day for a date, as the two of them really needed time alone, but I did decide having Glorian around would make my venture more interesting.

As we walked across the bridge to the main island, the elf kept to my side, his eyes wandering around the trees and what now I knew to be a forest city. buildings built into nature, making it look from a distance that it was mostly uninhabited, while in actuality, the Isle of Whitview was a bustling city, full of various creatures and races.

"Cool –" Glorian murmured, his eyes fixed on a tavern that had trees growing from the stone sides, thick natural vines making up a whole wall of the building, and a canopy of leaves mixed with boards of wood for the roof.

"Bloody brilliant isn't it?" I grinned, looking down at him. "When I was here several years ago, it was a prominently human land. Looks like the Mystics and Fae have taken her back."

"Or learned to work together," the blue-skinned elf pointed, my eyes following his finger to another half-stone, half-nature-formed building that seemed to be a library. This library was formed of a giant oak, that stone had been built around, branches between the stones and around the tall glass windows as a natural frame. I wanted to cry with joy, while I may be a sailor – I have always loved the forest – and people.

As we continued to walk through the town, I realized Glorian was right. All of the buildings looked like a cross between humans and nature made, a balance between what is natural and what is created. It was breathtaking, each building strikingly different than the last, some of them painted and others wood and stone.

"It looks Fae," Glorian remarked, his eyes trailing back to me. "There are also a lot of Fae here –" he eyed a group of notably Fae girls as we walked.

I paused in my tracks, turning to the most Fae-looking of the girls. She had long purple hair that turned into a tail at the end, somewhat reminiscent of a demon tail, thin with a pointed end. Her skin was a deep indigo, making her hair look paler than it was. Her eyes were a solid pale blue, and when I spoke a swift "Hey" to her, those eyes seemed to peer into my soul, and I felt my face go red. Her black lips pursed as she looked at me, a brow raised.

"Hello?" Her voice was smooth and wispy, like a soft breeze in summer. My ears trembled as my heart cooed, my eyes widening. She held her hand out to shake, and I immediately took it, leaning down to kiss her clawed hand.

"I must have been at sea for way too long, for surely something as beautiful as you could only be a figment of my imagination." I kept my body low, looking up to her. "What is your favorite drink, beautiful? Because I would love to buy you one tonight."

Her face turned from indigo to purple, her fawn-like ears lowering with embarrassment, and I could hear her heartbeat begin to speed up. I knew I was in – or, would have been if Glorian hadn't smacked my hard across the head, just as the Fae was about to reply.

"Blaidd!" Glorian hit me again, grabbing onto my hand and beginning to walk with determination.

"What –" I was tempted to grab onto his ear and throw him to the ground. For the sake of begging a gentleman in front of the ladies, I kept myself composed.

"We don't have time –" he glanced at the Fae, before looking back at me, eyebrows raised.

"We have plenty of time –" I was going to beat the runt – I was. When I looked back at the boy, however, there was a warning glance in his eyes, as if he knew something I didn't. I glanced back at the indigo girl, then back to Glorian.

"But –"

"Trust me –" He nearly growled, and this time, I decided to listen. It wasn't worth the public fight that would likely scare the girls away, besides, there was a fear in the moon elf's eyes that told me he was helping me somehow. I glanced back at the girls one more time, a pout on my face.

"But –"

"Blaidd Delphire."

"Fine –" I turned back to face the Fae, nodding to the indigo Fae specifically. "I'm sorry, my dear – but my companion is right –"

She frowned, her friends moving to comfort her. "Will we meet again?"

"I do not know my love." I kissed her hand again, and with that, Glorian pulled me away, finally forcing a distance between the Fae and myself. She lifted her hand, waving slightly. I did the same.

After we were a reasonable distance, I turned to Glorian, my eyes asking my question for me. "What was that about?"

"She was Unseele, most likely some type of shade from the night court."

"And?" I prompted.

"She would have eaten you –"

"..." I pursed my lips.

"I mean LITERALLY have eaten you, Blaidd –"

I stayed silent for a long moment as we walked, glancing back, the Fae gone at this point. I looked ahead of me. "In that case – thank you." I nodded. "But I can protect myself, you know."

"Clearly not. Also, The one you were talking to, if she was a shade- she was not a she. Female shades have blue skin, not indigo."

"..." I pursed my lips again for a long moment, then shrugged. Glorian just shook his head, looking back ahead. He was clearly mad, although I had trouble figuring out what about. I hadn't gotten hurt, and he was fine. I also could have defended myself. While I was a flirt, I was far from dumb and kept steel on myself in case a fae ever did try to eat me.

We walked for some time, surveying the buildings for any signs or anything that made the buildings stand out as a tradepost. Glorian was extremely quiet, and he was clearly still thinking about the interaction with the fae. Eventually, he seemed to not be able to stand the silence and spoke.

"Are you really that lonely?" His question caught me off guard and was not quite what I had thought he was going to ask. When I didn't answer right away, the elf looked up to me, his gaze focused.

"Lonely?" I scoffed, rolling my eyes, "I'm not a lonely Glorian." I laughed.

"Could have fooled me" The elf crossed his arms as we continued to walk. At these words I stopped walking, my ears falling back, my tail lowering to the ground. Glorian too stopped, turning to face me, his arms still crossed.

"I have the Outcast and her crew. My family. The crew is my family." I laughed again, shaking my head, despite knowing my body language gave away my true thoughts. "How could I, of all people, feel lonely?" I placed my hands on my hips, tail flicking.

"I see the way you look at Val and Beck when they are together."

"They are leaving the crew in a few months. Of Course, I'm sad when I see them, knowing that they are leaving. Beckett is my best friend." I laughed again, no real amusement in my tone. Beckett had informed me he and Val intended to leave and start a family in less than a year, and I didnt blame them. It hurt, knowing my two best friends were leaving, but I knew I would manage.

"That's not what I mean and you know it."

"Why do you feel like you need to know everything about me, Asterin? I am your captain, and I tell you what I wish. You have no business being in my- business!" I finally snapped, The boy took a step away from me. I could tell he was taken aback by my use of his real name, and I watched as his hands balled into fists.

"You seem to be able to ask what you want about me- Besides, *Romulus-*" He barely got my name out when I was on top of him, grabbing onto his collar and lifting him above the ground.

"Besides what-" I growled lowly, my ears flat to the back of my head, and my body tense, ready to throw him to the ground and attack before he had a chance to fight back.

Glorian kept his eyes focused on mine, despite his wide-eyed fear. "I'm trying to be your friend-" He spoke with determination, his eyes softening as my anger switched to sadness. I lowered him slowly, letting go of his collar once he was on the ground.

"Some friend." I scoffed, refusing to look at the boy. After a moment he spoke again.

"You are not exactly friendly to me you know,-" he started "But I can tell you need someone- besides... I know your secret."

That finally made me look at him, tail twitching. "And what secret is that?"

"The secret hat you're only a year older than me, despite looking like you are in your twenties. The secret that you left home when you were a child and lived in Faerie for years before leaving and coming to Eritis. The secret is that you cry yourself to sleep every night, because even though you left willingly, you wanted to go back, but realized you were lost and couldn't find your way back home. the secret that you miss your family, your mom, brothers and sisters, and most of all, your twin brother; and how it kills you inside that you left. The secret that the outcast started out as a vessel to find your way home, and how you already decided if you ever find out where you are from, you will go back, but deep down, you know

you will never find your home, because that day
you crossed into faerie, there was no going back.”

The longer he spoke the more I regretted
letting Glorian go, and wanted to slap him, or
strangle him, or just kill him plainly, but my mouth
was dry, and for one of the few times in my life, I
didn't know what to say to him. I felt my heart race,
and slink in a pattern as I tried to decide how to
feel. “how do you-”

“I found your diary.” His gaze stayed fixed
on mine. In reality, when I wanted to scream at
him, I wasn't even mad. A mix of emotions spun
through my mind, but more than any there was a
sense of relief that he knew. I knew his story, so it
was only fair.

“Is that why you hate your name so much?”
he asked, eyes still on me.

I stayed silent for a while, before meeting
his gaze. “aye.” I looked away. “Going by a different

name...well, It makes it...hurt less." I smiled forcibly, knowing how fake it looked. "We should get going, if you aren't going to run away that is." I took a step, pausing to glance back at the elf. While I could tell he wanted to talk more, I was done. Even now I wanted to shrink into a little ball and hide in my cabin and cry relentlessly, but we had stuff to do, and crying in front of people was not something I did.

"Nah, I think we've had enough of that..." Glorian began to walk, matching my pace at my side. I smiled a little more genuinely that time.

After some time of walking in silence, the elf looked up at me, his brows furrowed in thought and confusion. "Wait if you lived in Faerie there is no way you didn't know that was a guy!"

Parc Six

Purple walls, Chirping frogs, and Grumpy Goblins.

It took another twenty minutes to finally find the small purple-painted building with a small wooden sign that hung above the open-fronted building, labeled 'Mollies'. Glorian and I looked at one another, and while I tried not to expect things, it was still not what I had been expecting. The building was crowded, and what I thought was an open front was in fact a porch littered with various items that were either too big to fit outside or intended for outdoor use. Colorful Canoes and lamp posts, wind chimes, and lawn ornaments.

As we walked past I ran my hand along the windchimes that were strung along the edge of the leafy porch roof, chuckling at the sounds they made, as the different sizes and materials all made a wacky orchestra of dings, clunks, and doops. There was one chime that was definitely enchanted, as when I hit it, it sounded like a frog's croak. I grinned widely and began to tap at it repeatedly, and was pleasantly surprised when a small tree frog fell out of the chime and onto my hand.

"Oh, hello. I'm sorry I didn't mean to disturb you." I looked at the frog, my amber eyes surveying the green slimy creature. Its big black eyes focused on me, then after a moment croaked loudly.

"oh, well, that's good then I suppose."

The frog croaked again.

"Oh dear- she didn't-"

CCCrrroak

"Oh, my word. Well while I agree with you, you shouldn't use such language." I frowned and only then realized Glorian had paused to watch the interaction, his brows furrowed in a look of absolute confusion.

"There are children here" I leaned to the frog, whispering slightly, my eyes on Glorian.

"We just went over this! You are only a year older than me!"

"He's sensitive-" I ignored the elf, continuing to speak to my new friend.

"I am not?!" Glorian snapped- then paused. "Why do I even try- you talking to a frog for Grace sake!" With that, he turned and pulled open the wooden door to the shop, and went inside, a monotony of different bells dinging. I looked back at the frog, and he croaked again loudly.

"Are you sure? I am a sailor, and-"

CCCRRROOOAAKK

"Oh, I see." With his words, I placed the small green frog on top of my head and between my ears. He immediately snuggled in my curls, and I followed Glorian into the trading post.

The inside of the post was more fun than the outside. Fuller then full of various items. Pieces of furniture, rows of clothing, bookshelves full of various items, the books themself on stacks in the corner of the room, nearly reaching the ceiling. Various ornaments were hanging from the short wooden ceiling to the point that I had to crouch. Chandeliers and wall hangings, rows of paintings on wires and chains jewelry and kites, and what really seemed to be anything and everything that could hang. Near the door was a glass case of unorganized piles of jewelry, with a pile of various weapons leaning against the wall.

I touched basically everything I could the moment I stepped in the door, my eyes wide with excitement at all the things around me, lifting my hand and letting it graze across the various bobs that hung from the ceiling, my ear almost immediately getting snagged on a wooden wall hanging in the shape of a goose.

"Careful!" a small croaking voice caused me to turn to the counter, and the small man behind it, of whom I had not seen a moment before. He was small, with olive green skin and only a few strands of white hair peeking out of his head and long pointed ears. His black eyes focused on me, and I grinned at the man, of whom I knew to be a goblin. Glorian looked over as well, practically jumping when the goblin spoke. so he hadn't seen him either.

"If you break stuff then I have to lower the price, and the lower the price the less gold, and the less gold the more problems-" He rolled his eyes, then focused his soulless eyes on me. "Keep those ears and that tail in check, or I'll throw you out girly."

"I'm not-"

"Do I look like a care girl? I get ya Fae in here all the time, and I can't tell ya apart anymore, so if I say you're a girl then you're a girl." He grumbled, looking away from me as he spoke, looking down and organizing the jewelry case- or, well, that's what looked like he was trying to do; in reality, he seemed to be taking what little organization there was and ruining it.

"Are you Mollie?" Glorian glanced at me, then his silver eyes set on the goblin.

"MOLE- Ey. It pronounced Mole-ey you little-" The goblin looked up, all but growling at Glorian. I stifled a laugh.

The hairless goblin turned his eyes to me, "What's so funny wh-"

"WOE-" Glorian leaned forward, slamming his hand against the case in front of Mollie. "Don't you DARE talk to my captain like that!" The elf's silver hair fell in front of him, sliding out of the leather chord it was pulled back in.

"Aww I love you too" I pursed my lips at his words, a little flattered, given how many times in the past month Glorian had tried to jump ship. to still refer to me as his captain almost made me blush.

"Capt-" Mollie looked at Glorian, his eyes narrowing for a moment, then working with realization. "ah, so you are one of them merchant ships? In that case-" I felt Mollie's businessgoblin starting to develop. "Anything in the store is yours, granted yo-"

"We aren't merchants." I leaned against the counter, getting a sneer from the goblin.

"Oh yeah- then what are ya?" he narrowed his eyes, leaning closer to my face, I grinned wide, blinking at him twice before speaking. "Mercenaries." I raised my eyebrows.

Mollie immediately took several steps back, and I saw his hand reach for one of the shortswords that rested against the corner. My eyes wandered briefly, resting on an intricately detailed knife tied to a small perfume bottle. It appeared to be a set, the same floral detailing on the knife handle as the pink glass perfume bottle.

"What- what do you want with me?" Mollie's words snapped me back to reality, and I turned my attention back to him.

"We have heard tale that you have a map that leads to something I need." I leaned forwards just slightly, and Mollie lifted the sword, pointing it directly between my eyes.

"Map?" His eyes narrowed, and I could see Glorian also looking at me in confusion. I hadn't fully told him or the rest of the crew exactly what was going on, and then realized that he probably assumed that my quest from Mogotsi was to end here. In an instant I pushed Mollie's sword, pulling mine from its sheath and immediately disarming him, Glorian fumbling to catch the shortsword, his eyes wide with horror as he managed to not cut himself, catching the sword messily in his arms.

"I don't want to cause a fight." I signed as the goblin reached for another sword, moving my blade in front of him, making him pause. "Do you know of the map to the Harbinger stone?" I kept my eyes on him, sighing slightly as I spoke.

"I might," he growled, eyeing my blade.

"I need it, and I'm willing to pay handsomely."

"You pull a sword in my shop and expect me to help you?" Mollie snapped.

"You pulled a sword on me first" I raised an eyebrow.

CCROOAK

I had forgotten he was up there.

Mollie looked up at my head, confusion growing on his angry face. I lifted my sword, eyeing him closely, then slid it back, and resheathed it. Glorian looked at me, frowning, still holding the short sword in his arms like it was his firstborn son.

"I don't want to fight, I just want the map" I repeated looking at Mollie, tilting my head. He grumbled some choice words directed at me- likely not knowing I would be able to hear, or maybe he didn't care.

"We know you have it, you know you have it, can't we make this fair and easy? " Glorian prompted, lowering his sword baby till he held it how a sword was supposed to be held, blade pointed at the ground.

Mollie paced back and forth for a moment, mumbling words even I couldn't understand, then paused across from me. I rested my head in my hands, leaning against the counter again. I blinked repeatedly at him, trying to make my eyelashes and beautiful big eyes convince the goblin. I think I scared him more, as he backed away further. Rude.

"A deal" he glowered at me. "You do something for me, and I'll give you the map"

My insides started reeling and not in a good way, more like when you eat a piece of tree bark and it goes down the wrong pipe and you start wondering if you are going to have a tree lung baby, but then realize you're not just not ready for parenthood. But have no idea how to raise a tree baby but know you couldn't give the tree baby up for adoption because that's your baby and you the father and you couldn't love anything more than that tree baby- but being a single parent is hard but you can do it because you are a strong independent man- only to find out it didn't go down the wrong pipe and you just overreacted, but now your sad because you were ready to be a parent....kind of reeling.

"and you pay for it" he added before I got the chance to ask how much it would cost. Glorian and I looked at each other for a long moment, the elf gave me a 'seems fair' kinda glance. My brows furrowed as I grinned, and I turned back to the goblin.

"Let me see it first" My tone was more demanding than I had intended, but I decided to go with it, my gaze still fixed on Mollie. The few hairs on his head seemed to stand up in annoyance, as if he was trying to make himself bigger to intimidate, the goblin being half my height however, did little to nothing to sway my decision to see the map. I raised an eyebrow in waiting.

"How do I know you ain't going to steal it before the deal is done?" He grumbled.

"We need proof you have it," Glorian explained. I nodded in agreement.

"You two dummies don't even know what I want done-" he lectured, but none less leaned down and pulled a rolled piece of parchment from under his display case, his gnarled fingers still gripping it as he set it down on top of the glass, pulling at the ribbon to open the thing. My eyes stayed trained on the map as he did so, feeling my insides flutter as the parchment was unrolled to reveal exactly what he had said it was. A map, with old, cursive writing at the top that made it clear this in fact was the map the King of Shadows had spoken to me about.

I leaned to get a better look at the writing, but as I did, Mollie snatched it away, rolling it back up and hugging the rolled map to his chest.

"There. You see I have it, now, your end of the deal" he glared at me, as if leaning to look at the map was some type of unredeemable sin. My fists clenched, one of my rings digging into my pawm, causing me to clench my jaw.

"Right-"

Croak

"... Is there a frog in your hair?" Glorian turned to look at me, a gaze of bewilderment in his gray eyes.

I pursed my lips, looking at the Elf, blinking innocently.

"That's the second time you've croaked."

"Of course, there is a frog in my hair, don't ask silly questions, Glorian. You should know better by now."

"... Is it the same one as outside? "

"Yes. He dreams of adventure, and freedom from an abusive relationship"

"... Why did I ask-" he paused, brows furrowed "So you... actually can understand them?"

"Excuse me!" Mollie grumbled. "I love the fact that you two are crazy-" there was no love in his tone "but do you want my map or not?"

"Yes," I smiled, leaning on the counter again, head in hands, tail swaying-crashing into several items in the store in the process. Mollie's eyes twitched. Both of them. Quite frankly I was unaware that was possible.

"Good." He frowned "My daughter ran away, and no matter what I do I can't convince her to come back, no matter how much I try, she refuses!"

"I can't imagine anyone not listening to you, you're so kind!" I commented. Glorian elbowed me hard in the stomach.

"I know! I don't understand it myself" he murmured, nodding to me. "She's only 215! She doesn't understand how dangerous it is for her to leave! She is so young. "

"Incredibly young. " I nodded, my ears flopping. Glorian also nodded. I don't know about the aging of goblins, but from what I heard their lifespans weren't that long- at all. Maybe he just didn't know quite how time worked. I made a note of that, in case we were gone for more than an hour to get his daughter, and came back a hundred years later.

"Did the two of you get into a fight?" I was a little annoyed that Glorian asked, but at the same time thankful I wasn't the one to have done it.

"Of course not!" Mollie grumbled. "She just left and refused to come back when I did find her. You two seem like you know how to talk, so talk her back into coming home, for me, and the map is yours-" He frowned deeply, and I began to wonder if his daughter was actually a cat. Cats did that sometimes, and maybe she just wanted some fish, instead of begging and talking into coming home. Fish usually worked, not that I have had a cat.

"oh, he's very good at talking." Glorian glanced at me, then looked to Mollie.That deserved a good toss off the ship when we got back. A nice far one where he would actually have to swim to get back on board. I smiled to myself.

"That I am" I bowed, deciding to tell Glorian about my plans to throw him out later. Mollie grunted with a nod.

"And we here might find your daughter? And what is her name of course? " I straightened myself, wanting to get moving. The smell of old stuff had already ingrained itself into my nostrils, as well as something that smelled like dying sunshine. Or maybe it was just Mollie who I was smelling.

"Her name is Lydia. Dark hair, fair skin. A little thing. She's been staying at the town inn. Big spruce building." I nodded as Mollie spoke, and after a small word of conversation, Glorian and I left without a wave, going to find Lydia.

Part Seven

Iye, Fiddle me timbers - The dance of a princess is to swoon.

Where's me Elf?!

I was very glad to realize that Glorian and I had passed the inn on our way to Mollies, making it significantly easier to find than the goods store had been. It was about a twenty-minute walk, and as we did so, something that had happened in Mollies kept entering my mind, a nagging feeling like an itch on my pawm. I glanced at Glorian, who was keeping pace beside me. My ears lowered slightly, tail swaying when he seemed to realize I was looking at him and looked over. The elves' brows furrowed in confussion- an expression I was beginning to think was his trademark- as he eyed me.

"What?" He questioned, slowing his pace slightly. I did the same.

"You don't know how to sword fight, do you? When we were in mollies and I tossed you that sword, you acted like you had never held one before." I frowned, my hand on the hilt of my rapier. Glorians eyes trailed to my hand, then down the blade at my side.

"I don't." He admitted. "I know how to use throwing knives, but not a sword." His eyes still landed on my sword, his face flushing with slight embarrassment.

"Well, we can't have that. Not if you're part of my Crew. no no, swordplay is a requirement." I looked at him, ceasing my walking in front of a tea shop, arms crossed. "That is if you intend to stay..." I raised an eyebrow.

The elves' eyes widened, looking at me in shock. "What?"

"It's been four months Glorian-" I grimaced. "That's long enough. I'll miss ya, but I'm not going to make you stay any longer than you have to. Your ransom has been paid in full, for the service you have done for me and my ship. "

"I don't want to go-" he frowned. I was unable to stop myself from smiling.

"Good. " I smiled "So what I saw saying-" I started walking again, " if you are staying, swordplay is a req-" I paused realizing my friend was not following and did not turn to face him, my hand up a small wave motioning for him to follow. "Come on-" After a moment the sound of footsteps making their way to me began, and I was met with Glorians teary eyed smile when I looked to my left.

"So we definitely think it's a cat, right?" I offered

"Oh definitely-"

We reached the inn within a few more steps and made our way inside. There was no door, much like several of the other buildings, but an entrance made of wooden vines that grew in the shape of a snaking arch in a Z shape, like a small hidden entrance Hall instead of a door. Clever. I ran my hand against the vines, a resting smile on my face as I traced the twisting and intersecting vines till we made it inside the inn.

Once inside, it was evident this was not just an inn, but a tavern of sorts as well. Despite it being the day, the inside was crowded, with all sorts of fae, mystics, and Humans inside, talking, eating, and drinking at the bar. A small stage sat in between two spiral staircases leading up, where a small band of pixies played, filling the air with the music of the fae folk. Glorian looked at me, clearly nervous, and looking as if he too was beginning to suspect maybe Mollie's daughter wasn't a cat. Part of me wished she was, it would make bringing her back home so much easier.

I was unable to stop a wide grin from spreading on my face, however, when I took in the sight of the inside. The music, the people, the dancing, it was a cheerful environment and one I knew I thrived in. My eyes fixed on a dark-haired gal who seemed to be some type of half-elf, talking to a blonde-haired Fae at the bar. While there was nothing that stood out about her in the crowd, something told me I should go talk to her. She wore traveler's clothing, which piqued my interest more than a little. Leather armor with bags draped over her skirts, a sword at her side, and a small knife that I could just see sticking up, pushing her burgundy dress top causing the fabric to sway in a movement opposite of the way the rest of the fabric fell.

I knew keeping focus was more important, and as I turned around to face my blue-skinned friend, only to realize he was gone-and I was startled to hear my name being called from the crowd.

"Blaidd!" A cheerful male tone called, causing my head to whip around so fast I thought my ears were going to fall off. I was met with the sight of a shorter man, a human, with blonde hair and brown eyes that glittered with a golden hue in the lights of the tavern. Sanador Dawson. I forced a smile onto my face, and not that it wasn't genuine, I just had a feeling about where this interaction was going to lead. A conversation of a time before the outcast, back when I was trying to figure out who I was and what I was supposed to do with my life.

"Heya Sandy!" My eyes were unable to focus on him as they darted around the tavern, trying to find my elf.

"How have you been?" He smiled brightly "I haven't seen you since the wedding!" He pauses for a moment, his eyes sparkling. "Do you still play?" With that, he had my attention. I was unable to stop the toothy grin that spread across my lips as I bowed slightly.

"But of course. " I fixed my eyes back on him as I straightened myself. "Although I do not fancy myself much a bard these days."

"Oh! Well, that's a shame!" Sandy frowned "You are one of the best I have ever heard, especially with that fiddle of yours! You do not understand the honor it was to have you play for my wife and I."

Glorian. Glorian. I had to find Glorian and we had to find the non-cat goblin daughter. My tail flinched as I struggled to not get pulled into the conversation.

"Here's a thought!" Sandy's voice interrupted *my thoughts*. "How about I buy you a drink, and you can play something here for us! I know the owners of the inn, I can get you whatever you need to play."

My ears shuttered at the thought of getting to play in front of a crowd again. I had played for my crew before, in fact, it wasn't uncommon, and while I cherished those moments, the thrill I got from playing for a crowd was more than I could bear. The joy it brought people, seeing them get closer through the music I made, had always warmed my heart, and in many ways, was something I lived for. When our eyes met, I could tell Sandy could sense that I more than wanted to.

"Any drink you want. Just one song."

It was not just one song, nor was it one drink. After my first drink, Sandy managed to convince one of the musicians to let me play their violin, and when I picked up the instrument, my mind went blank, and I got lost in the music. Several songs and several drinks later my mind was only focused on the instrument in my hand and the sounds it made. The people in the tavern danced and clapped along to the upbeat tunes I played, making the air around full of excitement and thrill. When I would even attempt to stop the patrons in the tavern would ebb me on, and I barely noticed as the night began to fall.

As the day dragged on, The brown-haired girl made her way to the front of the stage to watch me, a smile on her face,as all around her clapped and danced. Anyone with any form of instrument playing along as I let my magic flow with the music. Her brown eyes glittered in the light as she made eye contact with me, my already large smile growing. I jumped down from the small stage, somewhat bowing to her as I glided the bow against the strings.

"Are you trying to impress me, bard?" I could barely hear her over the excitement in the room, but I could make out her words and strong ladylike voice that I got the feeling I would not want to cross, or I would get something thrown at me. She bore an accent from the south, and it was easy enough to tell she was not from around here. Then again, her clothing had already said that.

"That depends. Is that something you would like me to do, princess?!" I chimed in with the music around, then began to laugh. She laughed too. I took a few paces, taking a step around her before bowing again, still intently playing. My tail swayed, the plume on the end gently brushing against her skirt. She turned, understanding the meaning. Dance with me.

I was pleasantly surprised when the girl began to move in motion with me, and together we danced and for some time at that, well, the best we could for my being the lead in the music. I surveyed every inch of her as we moved in an unmatchable unison, each of us able to predict the movements of the other as if we had known each other for years, and danced together often. Step for step, sway for sway, and movement for movement. My smile only wavered when I heard my name being called, and spotted my elf pushing his way through the crowd calling my name on repeat.

"Blaidd! Blaidd we have to go!" I could barely hear his voice from the music, and while there wasn't necessarily a look of panic on his face, it was focused, my music wavered, and I turned to the brown-haired beauty, bowing to her. She nodded, and as I leaped back up to the stage I made a point for my tail to brush against her hand. I felt as she moved her fingers, running them across the plume as it made contact with her hands.

I made eye contact with Glorian again from the stage, his gaze unwavering from me. Fine. I played for a moment more so the tune could end naturally, then took a bow. The crowd cheered and began calling for more. Instead of fighting, I laughed, shaking my head no as I placed the violin in the hands of the fae who had let me borrow it to begin with, and took a long step off the stage, making my way to Glorian.

As we exited the tavern The music picked back up, and I glanced back to see if I could find my dark-haired princess, but she was gone. "I hate you-" I sighed, looking at the ground, doing my best to keep the drink from my voice.

"That was genius!" Glorian started. I definitely didn't think he had heard what I had just said; maybe I had only thought I had spoken. "Playing to draw everyone into the lobby! I found her within an hour, and we talked and well, she is going back!" Glorian smiled brightly, and I was happy to see the trace of the happiness I had spread via magic had caught The elf as well. He needed to smile more. As we made our way out of the tavern the bright pink of the sunset sky. Oops.

"You found her?" I glanced at Glorian, deciding that was not the best idea given my state, and focused my eyes back ahead of myself.

"Look!" Glorian smiled. Great. I mentally frowned. I was trying to not let the boy know just how far from sober I was, but he was not making it easy. I looked back over, eyeing the elf for a long moment before noticing the small winged girl that sat on his shoulders. She wore a simple white dress, no shoes, a black scarf, and black hair with four white moth-like wings sitting on her back. Her purple eyes focused up on me, a slight smile on the pixie's face.

"Hello!" she giggled. "I like your music Mr! You are very good" Lydia giggled again. I nodded a thanks to her, and after a brief introduction, made our way back to Mollies.

When we got back I wasn't sure quite how I felt about Mollie and Lydia's reunion, but I knew I was crying. A lot. My vision had blurred so much that I could barely hear when the Goblin explained that we did not pay for the map and that we could even pick something else to keep in the shop. Anything we wanted apart from jewelry. As Glorian had found her, and given my state, I let the boy pick an item. He grabbed his sword baby from earlier, and I couldn't have been more proud of a mother. I also let Glorian take the map, after I looked over it, making sure it was what we needed and was not being scammed. Not that reuniting a father and daughter was a bad thing, but we did need that map.

As we made our way out of Molies, Lydia waved goodbye, and as I glanced back I couldn't help but notice that, unless Mollie had cleaned in our absence-wich I highly doubted- The knife and perfume bottle from earlier were gone.

Land Ho!

(A relatively unintresting, yet important chapter)

We reached the Outcast before the sun was fully set, and now that my drink had fully begun to set in, Glorian led me most of the way, my head on top of his as we walked. I was happy he had decided to stay. Through the whole day the boy would have been able to run and disappear, and I probably never would have been able to find him, not if he wanted to stay hidden. While the isles were small, it was a lot of dense forests and cities, but Glorian had not just chosen to stay but helped find Lydia. Not quite the whole crew was back, which was about what I was expecting. Likely, despite what I had said, most of them would meander back tomorrow morning. As I stumbled onto the deck, passing Beckett on my way to my cabin, I murmured something that was supposed to be,

"I will discuss what our next heading will be tomorrow morning," but came out more like "I like your head, the morning next disgusting-" then began to uncontrollably laugh, my first mate chuckling as he switched places with Glorian, Beck Leading me to my cabin and helping me get ready for bed. I fell asleep immediately and quite frankly, didn't remember even reaching my cabin. I slept heavily and dreamless, I think I drank so much that even my dreams didn't seem to know how to work anymore, which, quite frankly, I was not entirely mad about.

When I woke up I had a pounding headache, sitting up in my bed, hands pressed against my forehead. My tail wrapped itself around my knees as I pushed them to my chest, silent. It was still night, my cabin dark apart from the light on deck that shone through the thin curtains over the window on my door, and the moon and starlight that glittered from the others. I got the feeling I hadn't slept over twenty-four hours, meaning it was still either early morning or night.

I looked through the dim light around the room, surveying the shelves and desk in my cabin, eyeing the roughly drawn pictures nailed beside my bed that held awful drawings of my family, or what

I could remember them looking like. I snapped my fingers, beginning a rhythm, then began to hum slightly. A bright orange magic, the same hue as my eyes, began to glitter in my hand in a smoke-like substance, kind of looking like an off type of fire. I used the light from the magic to help myself see in the dim light, pushing myself out of bed and grabbing my flint and steel, lighting my lantern, and sliding into the chair beside my desk. There my head fell on my desk, and I groaned loudly as the magic in my hand faded.

My head did not lift when I heard a knock at the door, just groaned again loudly in a 'come in.' I didn't look up past the figure that came in, assuming it to be Beckett. The sound of the breathing was off, and I could tell from the footsteps this was someone much smaller.

"Glorian?" I mumbled, lifting my head just enough to see the boy's blue skin.

"Hey." He smiled slightly, sitting down in the chair across the desk from where I sat. He eyed the mess, the piles of papers and maps, rolls of paper tied with colorful ribbons, my compass, pens and quills, bottles of ink, and a half-cleaned-up spill of crimson ink that looked a little more than suspicious. His eyes set on the ink for some time, before turning his gaze back to me.

"Why didn't you run away again- why are you here?" I mumbled, my brain was still fogged, and the moment I spoke I felt like I wanted to cry. Glorian must have sensed this, and grabbed a blanket off my bed, sliding it over my shoulders.

"Here's your map." He placed the paper down after making sure the blanket would not slide off my shoulders. I didn't want to look at it, the sight of paper making my ears hurt. I groaned again, sliding my head down till my forehead pressed against the wood of the desk.

"I looked it over, It seems…suspiciously straightforward. We just have to head to a lighthouse west of Raenmora, past the Monrothian mountains to a peninsula where there's an abandoned lighthouse, supposedly built in the first age, that's all the information on the map, an X on the lighthouse. The stone must be inside."

"You looked at my map."

"You were sleeping." Glorian raised an eyebrow, crossing his arms.

"My map-" I mumbled, looking at him, my fingers wrapping around the paper.

"Beckett set our heading while you were out"

"How long was it?!" I sat up, head pounding, regretting the moment immediately. I slammed my hands into my face, practically throwing the map down as I covered my eyes. I could hear Glorian trying to hold back a laugh.

"Around thirty hours." the elf mused.

"Thirty-" I repeated in a mumble "hours..." I paused for quite a while, letting my hands slide down my face till resting just below my eyes. Glorian stayed silent. "Why...do I- " I paused again, "still feel like.... Absolute-"

The door slammed open before I had time to finish, and I immediately grabbed my ears, pulling them down over my face, groaning loudly.

"Good morning sleepy head" Becket chimed a little full of energy for me at the moment, making me want to punch myself in the face. "I figured when Glorian didn't come back a few minutes after

I sent him to check on you, that must mean you woke up, finally."

"Finally-" I mumbled, wanting more than anything to crawl back into my bed and go back to sleep for another thirty hours. Beckett chuckled, and I did my best not to glare as I lifted my hands again. "How long till we get there-" I groaned, my head thumping back to my desk, which I was beginning to find quite comfortable.

"I thought you were the captain?" Beck mused, and I could hear glorian quietly trying to hold in a laugh.

"And you're my first mate, meaning you are supposed to do all the work *for me*." I adjusted so my chin was on the desk, eyes looking through my brow at my friends, who both stood over me kind of dauntingly. Well, Glorian was still sitting, but it still felt like I was in some type of trouble. Like when I used to get arrested weekly by the city guard in Dusted when I used to pickpocket from those who passed me on the street, or played my music to try and earn some coin in front of the palace- and the guards would group an in pairs of two or three after taking me to the jail, not in the cage but sitting me at a table, and lecturing me like the petty little boy that I was. A smile twitched onto my face, as it had back when I was that child, but instead of an assumed smile, with a nod and promise that I wouldn't do it again, knowing full well that I planned to the second I got out of that jail, this was a somewhat more genuine smile, knowing I was not in trouble this time, and that I was in the company of friends.

"Ok, seriously how long?"

We were seaborne for just over a week, what felt like a long journey to head back to just past where we had been only several days ago. Unfortunately, it was not entirely smooth sailing either, and this likely caused the lengthy journey. For half of the week, it rained on and off relentlessly, still for a few hours, then pounding rain and tall waves that threatened to knock the outcast down and under. We made it through, however, and the storm only motivated me to get the stone a little quicker. Not that the sea made me mad, I love her.

As I could see the land getting closer from the Outcast, I looked at it, a little too excited as I saw the trees and thick, lush forest we would have to enter in order to get to this abandoned lighthouse. While of course, Whitview was forest, the vivid greens of these trees and the knowledge that I would have to trek through them was exhilarating. While yes, the sea was my home, the peace I felt when lost in the brush of the forest was unmatched, and it had been so since I was a child. After a long day, running into the forests near my house and doing my best to get lost, just so I could feel safe in the shelter of the trees. It was a comfort, the same as the sound of the waves against the outcast at night, when all was still, the sunlight trickling through the leaves above, the sounds and symphony of the trees, animals, and plants made in the forest. If you didn't notice, I like the forest.

I sat up in the crow's nest, picking at the strings of a small lyre I usually kept with me, the memories of what had happened in the tavern washing over my mind. I hadn't realized how much I missed playing for a crowd, and I knew I needed to play for my crew more often.

Once the storm had cleared up, Beckett had proposed the idea of a crew dance to boost morale, and I had been more than open to the concept. Taking out the good food and drinks and letting those who knew how, to play together in a makeshift band made the moonlight deck alight with not just the stars but the laughter and joy that we all needed.

That had been the night before last, and the crew's mood had risen significantly. It only grew as the sight of land got closer, meaning we could not only stock the ship after our small feast but also get the stone and our gold.

I sighed, setting the instrument in my belt before making my way down. As I reached the deck, Crow smiled at me as he tried to tie his black hair back, the wind not doing him any favors.

"back to watch when you can." I chimed, and the boy nodded, sliding the feather that sat on the end of the leather he was using to tie his hair through a last loop, and with that, he made his way up. I had been thinking about who I wanted to take with me to get the stone and who I wanted to stay back and look for food, and I had to admit Crow had been high on my list of come-withs, as well as Beckett, Val, and for some reason, Glorian had kept coming to the forefront of my mind. Before he had volunteered to go with me to get the map, I hadn't even considered ever taking him with me, but he had proven he wasn't going to run, and while there was the forethought of possibility of him trying to steal the stone, I had come to trust the boy.

As if on cue, I looked over to see glorian looking at me, his gaze focused on the lyre on my hip. "hello, darlin'." I smiled.

"Darlin..?" Glorian furrowed his brow, clearly not finding my attempt at a joke funny.

"Never mind, I was just thinking about you." I smiled. Glorian grimaced.

"Should I find that comforting, or should I be worried?"

"I want you to come with me. To the lighthouse, to get the stone." my smile rested into a more genuine thing. "only if you want, of course."

"Me-" his eyes wanted to mine, our eyes locking. My smile widened as I nodded.

"You have been here through most of it. If you want to see it through, I want you to have that option."

Glorians arms moved in a motion to hug himself as the salt coated wind blew over us. After what felt like an eternity of waiting for an answer, he nodded. "yeah. Yeah, I'll go." he smiled, nodding. Again, my smile grew.

"Brilliant."

While I wanted Beckett to come with as well, by the time we made it to shore, it was decided that he should stay back and keep the crew under control as they looked for supplies. He and Val to be keeping track of what they needed and making sure everyone actually worked, at least for the most part. Once we made it to the small beach Glorian and gathered what we needed, I grabbed my sword, a flask full of water, a knife, and-

"Hey, Glorain!" I practically screamed out my cabin door, nearly jumping when I saw him leaning against the wall on the outside. "Oh, there ya'r," I snorted. he rolled his eyes. "Come here!" I grabbed him by the wrist, not giving him much choice for resistance.

I let him go after pulling him in and running to a chest that sat at the foot of my bed, kneeling and digging inside. "Since I didn't have much time to teach you swordplay because of the storm, and quite frankly, I don't know what we may encounter out there, you need to be prepared."

"You think we are going to have to fight?"

"It's a super rare magic stone with the power of a wishing star. I've been in this business long enough to know it can't be as easy as just walking up and picking it off the ground. While I don't want to fight anything if we don't have to, I want you to be prepared. These were made by a blacksmith I once helped; I don't have much use for them; I thought you may find them, well, useful." As I spoke, I dug through, eventually finding the roll of leather that made up a belt with a small bag on the side, messily shoving everything back into the trunk before turning to my blue-skinned friend.

"For you." I grinned, holding out the belt to Glorian. After eyeing it for some time as if thinking this was a trick, the elf reached out, grabbing the belt. I watched as he unclasped the pouch and pulled out one of the blades.

"Throwing knives." he turned the steel arrowhead-shaped knife over in his hand.

"There's only twelve, so don't lose them."

"How did you know I use-"

"You told me. When I got you your sword-baby, you said you didn't know swordplay but knew how to use throwing knives."

"...Oh yeah," he muttered, looking back down at the blade. "thank you-" his eyes trailed back up to mine looking as if he was still expecting this to be some kind of trick.

"Of course, kid." I pat his head smiling, "Now let's go! We have a Harbinger stone to get."

We separated from the crew, leaving while the rest prepared for their tasks. I waved to Beck, letting him know we were off, and with that, Glorian and I made our way onto the small beach and into the thick forest. I pulled out our map almost immediately, followed by the compass on a chain on my belt. "Fortunately, it is an old lighthouse; unfortunately, we couldn't see it from the coast, so all we had was the map to help lead the way."

"Do you think there is a chance the land formations could have changed at all? I would think we should have been able to see a lighthouse from the coast, abandoned or not."

"I have a feeling it's hiding in the trees, up there." I looked up from the map, holding the hand that held my compass up, my eyes following.

I was facing the end of the peninsula, which was up on a cliff, an ideal spot for a lighthouse. Due to the cliff edge around it and the sharp rocks that lined it's face, it was apparent why we couldn't have just climbed up that way. We would have to trek through the forest for what I guessed would be a few hours. Glorians eyes followed mine, and he nodded. With that, we began to walk.

The smell of the forest the second we arrived at the treeline made me all but have to force myself to keep on task. The same urges from my childhood to run into the forest washed over me, the urges that had gotten me lost and in faerie to begin with. I started to hum myself, letting the dappled light from the trees graze my skin, my voice harmonizing with the birds and plants that sang around me as we walked along a dip that fell into the forest.

"What are they saying?" Glorians voice snapped me back to reality, and my ear fell in his direction.

"Hmm?" I blinked, ending my tune on a G.

"The trees and plants. You said you can understand them, so what are they saying?"

"I thought you didn't believe me?" I was unable to hold back a grin. The elf shrugged.

"I'm starting to think you're not as crazy as I thought." he shrugged.

"Don't be too-" Before I had a chance to finish my sentence, however, a strong force plowed into me, knocking me into a tree and causing me to stumble down the embankment Glorian and I had been walking along, the force falling with me.

ACT THREE

ᴘᴀʀᴛ Nɪɴᴇ

Honeysuckle and tree abuse

I wrestled with my attacker as we fell down the embankment and deeper into the forest, trying to grab my knife as my attacker made it clear she did not jump me because she wanted a hug. my back crashed into a rock as we reached the bottom of the embankment, falling into a bush of blooming small yellow flowers. As she pushed against me, we fought like wild animals, rolling and clawing against one another. I pushed myself up, weight pressing down onto her shoulders and forcing myself on top of my attacker. My eyes widened as they met the warm brown eyes of the traveler from the tavern; of whom I had danced with. Her wavy hair lay in a mess on the grass and flowers below, and a bruise was swelling on her face as she glowered at me.

"Honeysuckle?" I couldn't help but smile- although it fell quickly, the realization that she had just attacked me washed over my mind. Before I had the time to say anything else, her knee jabbed between my legs, causing a wave of pain that I couldn't ignore no matter how hard I wanted. The brunette took the moment of weakness to force me off of her, flipping the two of us and grabbing a knife, holding it to my throat.

"Excuse me?!" She snapped,

"The flowers?" I snorted.

Her eyes fixed on me for a long moment, and I could swear I saw red in her cheeks. After some time she tensed further, adjusting herself slightly. "Give it without a fight and I won't slice your neck open." She growled, her eyes darting to the map that was tightly grasped in my hand.

"My map?" My voice was higher than I had intended. That gave me an idea.

"Yes, the map! You are an idiot aren't you?" She pressed the knife closer to my neck. I did the best I could to pull it away from her, tilting my head to the side, still eyeing her closely.

"I never said I was smart" I mused, a smile resting back on my face. My hand around the map gripped tighter, and I pulled my arm away the best I could, given the fact that the girl was on top of me, one knee on my chest, the other on my arm. "But I must say- you are the one who hasn't taken it from me yet. It's right there, in my hand."

I spared a glance over to the map only to realize it had ripped during the fall, of course, the side of the map with the X missing. The girl also noted this. She eyed the map, the movement giving me just enough leverage to move, forcing the knife from my throat while her eyes were away. I let her take the torn piece of map for now, pushing up and kicking her back, and jumping to my paws. Instead of wasting the time to point my sword at her, I bolted, deciding to use sound to my advantage. My eyes began to glow as I started to back up the hill, amplifying the sounds of nature around to disorient her. Her incoherent yelling was enough for me to not have to take the time to look back to see if it was working.

As I pulled myself up, trying to ignore the sharp pain in my chest and gut, my ears twisted forward as I heard Glorian's voice in the distance well before I saw him. After a minute of hiking up the incline, I saw the blue-skinned elf making his way down to me, a piece of paper in hand. My eyes focused on the map, my magic fading as I lost my focus.

"NO! NO! OTHER WAY!" I bellowed, flailing my hands, trying to make him turn. Not that I thought moving my hands would magically make him move, but it was a funny thought nonetheless. After a moment of starring at me like a moth to a candle for several minutes, Glorian finally began to realize what I was implying. He stood still, looking down at the map, then at me, then behind me where I could hear the girl beginning to catch up.

"Oh- OH OH!" Glorian turned on his heel and began to run, the map tightly in his hand. As I moved to follow my companion, I felt a hand tighten around my tail and pull me down. The movement caused me to yelp rather unmanly and jolt back, wiping around to face the brunette, this time not hesitating to point my sword at her, my blade stopping only an inch in front of her nose.

"Let go of the tail love." My eyes focused on hers as my ears lowered behind me. "I would hate to scratch up that pretty face of yours-" As I stared at her, her eyes determined, I could see the echo of old scars across her face, barely noticeable, but still there nonetheless. "Any more" I added, raising a brow.

She let go, taking several steps back and pulling the rapier at her side, the silver blade nearly resting against mine. "I could care less about having a pretty face."

"So be it " I grinned, and with that, our blades began to clash. Just as with our dance several days ago, our movements were in sync, fluid together as if this was not our first duel. I gained one important piece of information from this: She not just knew what she was doing, but was experienced in swordplay.

We danced our way through the forest, the sound of steel clashing as we moved, my eyes determinedly fixed on her as we did so, a smile never leaving my face. "Why do you want the stone?" I questioned as I jumped up onto a low-hanging tree branch, taking several paces back. The girl jumped up, grabbing onto it with one hand and pulling herself up, her blade pointing at me.

"And why is that any of your business?" her eyes narrowed as her blade aimed directly for my head, I jumbled back, and onto a higher branch. I placed my sword handle in my mouth and jumped up, and onto a much larger and older tree, the forest now so dense and thick one could easily walk along the branches, the winding wood steady and constant, as if the nymph and fae often used it as a path.

"You tried to steal my map," I laughed, tail flicking. my claws fighting to dig into the branch beneath as I watched the brunette leap up onto the branch and stagger her way to me. "You're a wood elf?"

"And?"

"You are very heavy on your feet" I crouched as I waited for her to reach me. Sure I should keep going, catch up with Glorian, and leave her lost in the thick forest, but something stopped me. Let's call it curiosity. My eyes glittered slightly "Half-elf" I corrected myself

"But your other half isn't fully human now is it…" I tilted my head, taking a step back on the branch as she leaped onto it. Her brown eyes peered into me, her brows furrowed in a 'stop talking to me like we know each other, we are not friends' which personally I found offensive. Dancing together while both wasted is absolutely friendship.

"You talk a lot"

"Personally, I don't think you talk enough. Talking is the best way to get to know people, or not know them if the one talking happens to be a liar, but I suppose there is no point in talking much if one is a liar, or has something to hide, or maybe simply a private person uses their words sparingly. Are you a private person?" I blinked, lifting my blade.

The half-elves hands gripped tighter around the hilt of her sword. "What made you guess?" It wasn't really a question, and within a heartbeat, she swiped her blade at me. I dodged, the steel of my sword sliding against her blade, and with that, our duel commenced in the trees. Moving along the branches of the giant angelim tree we parried, step for step, till eventually, my back was nearly against the large trunk. She lurched her blade forward, and I veered to the side, the blade just barely missing my ear as it jabbed into the tree trunk.

"HEY!" I growled, "Dont hurt it!" My voice snapped, trembling as I pushed past the she-elf as tugged her blade out of the tree. We were now standing in reverse, the brunette against the trunk of the angelim.

"The tree!?" She glowered at me, although a string of confusion lined her face.

"Yes, the tree! He has no part in this fight! You had no cause to harm him!" As I shouted, it was as if the wind had blown, the branches of the tree creaking and moving ever so slightly, but there was no wind against my face. The brunette's eyes widened, glancing around at the tree and its winding branches.

"This is an ancient forest we tread, these trees undisturbed for centuries! And you attacked one!?" My tail twitched. She hadn't heard his cry of pain, the shock and wail of something so suddenly waking him from his slumber. The branches of the angelim continued to sway ever so slightly, and the look on my rival's face told me she was beginning to feel the ancient magic that she had just woken up in the forest.

"What are you?" She asked, her blade now pointing at me, warm brown eyes fixed on my amber irises. My anger for the old forest diminished as a smile spread across my face.

"Just a humble Bard" I bowed lowly, my eyes never breaking contact. She rolled her eyes, the blade of her sword following my nose.

"And your name?" she questioned, tensing as I straightened.

"Oh love, I can only tell you that, if you first tell me yours."

"Ridiculous" She took a step back, straightening her sword, the tip tapping against my own blade.

"What a silly name! " I mused, laughing slightly. "Although I do quite like unique names"

"Narissa-" she snapped, and I was unable to stop my grin.

"sea nymph?"

"Where I hail it means *one who creates an inspiring song*"

"Fancy" my tail swayed. I liked that name.

"And you? Now that I have told you mine it's only fair you do likewise? Unless you have no dignity in combat?" She de-tensed slightly as she spoke, and I knew if I was going to attack now would be the time, but something held me back. I could easily kill her. Blow out her eardrums and by simply manipulating the sound around us to cause her brain to explode-but, well, I don't kill.

"Blaidd!" I bowed, then before she had the time to react, jumped down and ran down the branches, sheathing my sword in the process. While the swordfight and banter had been fun, I had more important things to take care of.

"WOLF?!"

"YUP!" and with that I darted into the forest, in search of my elf.

Part Ten

Knock knock in the crystal cave

I darted through the woods as fast as my legs would take me, keeping my ears tuned for Glorian's voice or other footsteps that were not Narissa's. Even forcing myself to keep going after I had found a small group of humming mushrooms. If I was not worried about my elf, I definitely would have stopped. "That's not running!" I shouted when I finally spotted the elf's dark blue skin sitting on a fallen tree, holding the map tightly in his hands. He looked up, silver eyes glittering in the shadows of the trees.

"I got lost," the moon elf admitted, jumping to his feet as I got closer. He held the map out to me, and I immediately grabbed it, glancing around for a moment before my eyes fixed on the old piece of paper in my hands. My finger traced the map to the lighthouse down, my mind forming the missing half of the map.

"Here, we are right here," my finger rested off the map, down several inches past where it had ripped. "That means we need to—" my voice faded as I moved my finger up and toward the map, looking up again to find the sun. I pivoted my paw, tail pointing the way I was facing. "This way! Come on!" Without hesitation, I began to run, Glorian close behind me.

"What happened back there?"

"A not-so-old friend. She is after the stone as well."

"And do we have to run the whole way there?" He struggled to keep pace with me, falling a few steps behind almost immediately.

I jumped over a tree branch, my tail grazing the decaying wooden trunk. "Yes! I don't know if she followed me or not! She has the other half—" I stopped in my tracks, paws coming to a halt just in front of a small stream. From the corner of my eye, I saw Glorian catch up to me, stumbling at the sudden stop and just barely catching himself before falling into the stream.

"Well—" I mumbled, staring down at the map. As my eyes darted across it, I made sure to mentally note all landmarks, the direction of the lighthouse, and the coastline so if nothing else we could follow it back to the outcast. And with that, I crumpled the piece of old parchment and stuck it into my mouth. Glorian gawked at me, looking as if I had just done exactly what I just did.

"Grace help me—" He mumbled, still seemingly processing what had just happened. After a moment of pause, I chewed and swallowed the nasty old map, trying not to think too much about where it had been over the years. Molly's greasy old hands for one. It sorta tasted like tea that had been sitting out for days, with several dead bugs in it, and ginger instead of sugar was added. I made a mental note to maybe not do that again. I shook my head in disgust, then smiled encouragingly at Glorian, and began to run again.

After several miles, an old stone structure began to come into view. It was covered in moss and vines, but the base at least still stood, several feet off the ground, despite the fact that the top of the lighthouse was well destroyed. I slowed down my pace as we got closer, looking at the shell of what was once certainly a great building, the wooden door and window frames absent, leaving an eerie skeleton made of stone.

"So what? The stone is under a pile of rubble?" Glorian scoffed, and I had to admit I was just as uninterested in the idea of lifting bricks till we found the stone. I stepped over a small pile of stone through the large doorway, pausing when my eyes caught sight of some etchings along the frame. My hand lifted, my fingers tracing the now illegible script.

"I don't believe the destruction of this place was of natural causes." I half mumbled to myself. Glorian looked over, fear noticeable in his eyes. "You still have those knives I gave you, mate? Because I fear you may need them."

"I do," he nodded, hand resting subconsciously at his belt where the bag containing the blades lay.

"Good."

As the sun began to set, orange and gold light filled the sky. And with the distraction of light fading, I could feel the trace of an ancient magic just— "below us." My eyes widened. "It's under the lighthouse, not in it." Without a second thought, I began to shuffle around the debris, lifting and pulling at anything that could move. Without question, Glorian began to follow suit, the two of us now racing the sun to find some type of passage leading down.

"Blaidd!" Glorian called, running as he used all his force to push up a large piece of wall that had managed to stray together even in its fallen state. I ran over, helping him push and shove the wall. My eyes glittered as we managed to move it ,revealing a decaying wooden trap door, a faint light visible from the rustic boards of dark wood.

"And I don't even think we will need a torch!" I grinned, and without a second glance at the elf, pulled open the door and smiled down at the staircase below, various hues of blue glowing from below. I grabbed the sword at my belt and began to make my way down, my tail swaying behind me. As my paw touched the stone, I was shocked at how cold it was, given the fact that it was rather warm outside. Cold and damp. I began to make my way down the stairs, the cold dampness getting stronger as the world above faded. And while the light of the sun may have faded from view, the light itself did not. I glanced back to see if Glorian was following and smiled encouragingly at him when we made eye contact. He was not smiling back.

The steps began to fade to flat, a brick tunnel wide enough for Glorian and I to walk side by side if we wanted—but of course, the elf was hiding behind me. I couldn't blame him. We had no idea what we were walking into. My ears perked as a familiar sound rang in my ears, and my smile grew before I even saw the source of the glowing.

"Mushrooms?" Glorian's voice came from behind me, stepping around and walking up to one of the brightly glowing crystalline-looking mushrooms. He reached to grab it, before evidently deciding that was a bad idea. The walls were lined with the blue bioluminescent mushrooms, mingled together with moss and crystals from which the mushrooms and moss grew along and in some cases from.

The humming of the mushrooms, mixed with the small beats from the pulsing light of the crystals, and the gentle notes of the moss, all together created a pleasant sound. Coupled with the dim light, the space of the tunnel offered a relaxing environment. The longer we stood, the more I found myself not wanting to leave. I knew we had to, though. When I made eye contact with Glorian, we both seemed to have the same thought. Keep moving. We began to walk again, my hand brushing against the crystals and mushrooms lining the walls. I made a point to tap each of the larger crystals that protruded from the stone cave walls, not without pocketing a few mushrooms and smaller crystals as we walked, of course.

"I could live here," I hummed to no one in particular as we walked through the tunnels. Glorian glanced back at me where he stood a few paces ahead .

"You would die of starvation, and they would grow onto your corpse," he said.

"A blissful end." I chimed, pocketing another one of the smaller mushrooms. The mushrooms where odd, soft and airy as one would expect from a mushroom, however The second the mushrooms were separated from the cave, they would harden and become crystalline. Needless to say, my pockets got rather heavy quickly.

"You're so odd... and creepy. Oddly creepy." Glorian murmured.

"Now, odd I get, but what about me is creepy?" I ceased walking, my eyes fixed on my friend. His silver eyes glowed in the dark, his hair reflecting the blue light of the mushrooms and crystals around us.

"I think it's your eyes," he spoke after a considerable moment of silence.

"My eyes?" I blinked.

"Yeah – they are so... round and wide." He paused. "Every time I make eye contact with you, I feel like you're staring straight into my soul."

"You're weird," I snorted, and began to walk again. "I think we're almost at the end of the tunnel."

"I think it's how bright your eyes are compared to the rest of you too – I mean..." Glorian continued to ramble on about how unsettling my eyes were for the rest of the walk through the tunnel until we reached a large wooden door. The crystals and mushrooms seemed to have grown against the wood, so it's no surprise that when I tugged at the metal handle, the door barely budged. Glorian looked to me, and we adjusted side-by-side, both arms on the door, tugging to no avail.

After a considerable amount of sweat dripped down my face, I put my hands on my head in thought. My mind began to wander, thinking of ideas on how to break open the door. The crystalline growth had grown into the wood of the door, and their crystals certainly weren't made of sandstone. Crystal wood. Wooden crystals. Mushrooms. Glowing crystal mushrooms. Back to crystal. I frowned, pausing to stare at the door. It takes an axe to break wood, but even a hammer can't break diamonds. Crystal mushrooms. I blinked, mumbling to myself. "Magic humming mushroom rocks – hammers can't break diamond, no guarantee this is diamond, but not sandstone..."

"...What?" Glorian's eyes were still on me, his brow furrowed in confusion.

"Axes break wood, but an axe cannot break crystals," I said slowly as I moved to the door, looking at the crystals and mushrooms that coated it.

"Right...?"

"And what can break a crystal?" I spoke slowly as I moved to the door, looking at the crystals and mushrooms that coated it.

"A lot of things, I guess, but also very few... I doubt these are unbreakable, but still," Glorian murmured.

"So what cannot be broken can still be broken if itself was used to cause the damage. Like thoughts!"

"...Are you okay, Blaidd... like, up there?"

"You have to use the broken parts to break the unbroken!" I looked at him, eyes glittering as I smiled toothily, my hand sliding into my pocket. "Here!" I tossed the elf one of the crystalline mushrooms, Glorian just barely catching it. I eyed one of the crystals closely, a crystal mushroom in my own hand.

"I'm sorry, but I have to do this; I would, however, like to say you do make quite the lovely song, and I do hope this doesn't hurt you too much. Please don't scream." And with that, I took one of the crystal mushrooms from my pocket and began to use the cap like a small hammer, beating away at the crystal on the door. It began chipping away almost immediately.

Catching on rather quickly, Glorian began to do the same, instead using the sharper end of the mushroom to chip away at the crystal. As if by magic, this seemed to work. It took some time, banging the crystal against crystal, but we made progress. After breaking off a rather large piece, Glorian switched from his now-stump of a mushroom and used the long end to finish prying off the larger remaining chunks of the crystal from around the door.

"That should be good!" I stepped back, scooting a small piece of crystal away from the door. I wondered how much the crystal itself cost and what other magical properties it may have, but forced myself to shake off the thought for now.

"You don't suppose the stone will just be lying on the ground in there, do you? Like just sitting there, ready for us to grab without consequences?" Glorian eyed me.

"That is highly unlikely."

"I can hope right?"

"Yes, but – I have to imagine whoever hid it wanted it guarded. These crystals were just the first part of that guarding."

"Wait, you think it was intentional to have them grow onto the door?"

"In fact, I do." The two of us looked at each other for some time, my tail ticking with the seconds.

"Did he tell you who hid it?" the elf eyed me closely.

"He did not." I smiled.

"And you are sure you trust him?" he crossed his arms.

"I do. It is said the Harbinger stone can only be used by the pure of heart, and so he would have no use for it if his heart was not pure." My ear twitched, wanting to break open the door and stop this frivolous conversation.

"What if he has no heart at all?" Glorian mumbled, turning back to the door and positioning himself to yet again attempt to pull it open. I stood just above him doing the same. "If it's a dragon guarding that stone, one that's just cliché and disappointing, and two, I quit."

"Quit what?" I snorted.

"Yes."

"I think you have been spending too much time around me, mate." We both laughed for a brief moment before counting to three in unison and tugging at the door. We both pulled with our full strength, forcing the last of the crystal to make an unpleasant scratching sound. And within a moment, the door opened.

On the other side of the door stood darkness. No source of light, and even my eyes, which typically adapted to the darkness rather quickly, only saw the pure dark that stared back at me. "Here we go—" And without giving myself the thought to decide otherwise, I stepped into the darkness.

I could hear the sound of my heartbeat as I entered the shadow. A cold wash of unsettlement came over me as goosebumps began to line my arms. After a silent gulp, I snapped my fingers, the flow of amber magic alighting on my hand. The sound of the snap echoed through the space behind me. Even with the light, there wasn't much but darkness around that the light hit. I turned to look behind me, my eyes on Glorian, who looked past me, knife in hand.

"Can you see through it?"

"N-no."

"Alright." My tail swished. "This will be fun."

Making my way into the darkness, I did my best not to hesitate, holding a smile on my face as I hoped my eyes would adjust. Slowly and steadily, Glorian began to follow me, his footsteps echoing in what was evidently a large room. The light did little to nothing to help, and as I walked further into the room, I felt a heaviness on my chest that I didn't much like. It was as if a crushing weight was trying to suffocate me, and I struggled to breathe as the air grew thicker and thicker.

By instinct, I began to hum, a lowly ballad I had heard once in a tavern. I didn't realize how eerie it sounded until Glorian grabbed my arm and whispered a sharp, "Please stop."

I chuckled slightly, turning to my friend, just able to see him in the darkness. "What, do you think something is going to happen?" I stopped talking as a loud movement came from behind me, a shifting sound that sent my ears back. I realized something very large was moving infront of me.

Ꝓɑrꞔ Eleven

We fight - Uhhhhh

Immediately, I turned in the direction of the movement and squinted my eyes as the light came into the room. As the large beast moved, it brought to my realization that the room we stood in was shaped and detailed as though it were a throne room in a palace. large columns lined either side of the room, all leading up to a pedestal in the back where a statue of a small girl, adorned with four wings and two intersecting halos, stood, her hands together as if in prayer. She was surrounded by small windows near the ceiling where moonlight shone into the room. Because of the total darkness, the feint moonlight was enough to light up the entire room. It would have been an elegant view if it weren't for the large black beast that stood in front of me, its bright yellow eyes fixed on me.

The creature was large and covered in scales, with four large bat-like wings coated in scales and veins that gleamed through the moonlight. It only had two back legs, the front leg-like talons being a part of the foremost wings. Its face was stout, with tentacle-like tendrils from the sides, sticking out almost like horns, although the creature bore several horns on its head, smaller stout horns staring down at its jaw, hidden among the tendrils, and growing larger until reaching one longer horn in the center, almost like a crown.

Its eyes were all black, apart from the yellow pupils that glared back at me in either a reflective or glowing light. The creature's tail, long and narrow, with more tendrils and spikes than the tip, swayed almost playfully, as if it had found its new meal. Glorian and I were that meal.

My sword was in my hand before I realized it, braced and ready for combat. I was unable to stop the smile on my face as I saw Glorian move to my side, his knives in hand. I was not sure how much the small knives would actually do against a dragwyvdrawocky, but his courage was inspiring.

"What—is that—" The elf's voice was higher than a schoolgirl seeing a baby kitten cuddling with a bunny.

"I think I'm going to name it Uhhhhh."

"Uh?"

"No, Uhhhhh."

"What's the difference?!" He squeaked, then shook his head in realization of how ridiculous the argument was, given the fact that there was a large monster in front of us that in fact looked very hungry and very mad that we woke it up from its nap.

The dragwyvdrawocky, clearly not caring much about our conversation, let out an ear-piercing screech-like scream, which, I am sure even someone without super sensitive and enhanced hearing, would cause immense pain. I crumpled to my knees, my hands lifting to cover my ears the best that I could.

"HEY!" I screamed at the creature, and miraculously, it stopped. Making a grotesque, slimy-sounding clicking noise, more of a squelch than a click, but nonetheless, I was still shocked the creature stayed still as I straightened myself, steadily pushing myself back to my paws. I glanced to the side at Glorian, who was doing the same, muttering a quick, "You ok?"

"Yeah—" he whispered, standing up at the beast now that he regained his footing, knives still in hand. I gripped the blade of my rapier until my knuckles began to whiten.

"That wasn't very nice of you, you know. You shouldn't scream at people." I pointed the blade in front of me, but not up at Uhhhhh, as, for the moment, he seemed tame, and I didn't want to aggravate the creature into screaming at me again or attacking.

"What is happening—" Glorian mumbled as I tilted my head, the creature doing the same.

"I'm just saying, you aren't going to make many friends down here—and the rare occasion when people do come down, you are just going to scare them away. You don't want that, do you? I mean, you may look a little scary, but you must have a great personality, right?"

The creature moved, not to attack, just to adjust itself in front of the statue. Its massive wings half-covered the windows, making the room immediately darker. I knew there must be some type of magic filling the room that created the darkness, although I couldn't tell if it was from the beast or an enchantment on the room itself. Still braced for a fight, I took the time to look around the room, surveying it swiftly for any ways out, escape routes, or anything that could come into play if Uhhhhh decided to attack. Empty, as I had surveyed earlier, beyond the pillars that lined the walls and that statue. Was Uhhhhh guarding it?

Without much thought, I took a step forward, regretting it almost immediately as Uhhhhh let out a growl-like hissing sound, tensing and moving one of its clawed wings closer to me. Glorian took several steps back, and I placed a hand out in front of him by instinct. The creature let out that awful scream again, but this time I was prepared, using my magic to tone down the sound around Glorian and I, making it so that when the scream reached our ears, it sounded much more like we were underwater. Glorian looked at me, his eyes wide. I smiled wider.

The dragwyvdrawocky let out another scream, swatting its large clawed wing at the two of us, then lurching toward me with a snap of its jaw. I leaped up, jumping just in time to miss its large fangs, pushing Glorian away from me at the same time. The elf just barely caught himself as I bolted in the other direction, heading behind the pillars.

"I really don't want to fi- EEP!" I screamed as Uhhhhh swiped another claw at me, roaring loudly. This time he just barely missed, and that made me a little more than uncomfortable. I got the feeling he had decided not to be friends, which was sad and not just because I was hoping I wouldn't have to fight a dragwyvdrawocky to get a stone that may or may not be here.

It chased after me, and while I was glad to not have to worry about Glorian for the time being, having a big monster chasing me through the room was less than fun, although it was certainly exciting—just not that kind. I ran between the pillars in a weaving motion, heading towards the statue. Just as I thought I would be able to duck behind it, Uhhhhh used its large wings to fly above me, landing on the statue with another scream. This time an oil-like substance flung from the mouth of the creature, hitting the edge of my coat, which melted immediately. Acid.

"You may want to get that checked out," I frowned before turning on my heel, this time running straight toward one of the pillars, jumping onto it, and pushing onto the creature. I landed my sword straight in the shoulder of the beast. It let out another scream, lurching back and slamming me hard into the statue before knocking me off. I tumbled to the ground, wincing as I tried to push myself up, realizing I had landed on my left shin a little harder than I thought. I clenched my jaw, forcing myself up when the beast let out another scream. Thinking it was about to attack me, I looked up, surprised to see it recoiling off the statue, one of Glorian's knives in its eye.

I laughed with relief as the Moon elf ran over to me, helping me up and leading me to behind one of the pillars. "You ok?" He frowned, his eyes on me.

"Yeah, I'm fine—" I didn't speak until after putting pressure on my leg, and while it did hurt, I could still move fine.

"We should go—the door—"

"No—" I interrupted before he could finish. I ran a hand through my hair, making an attempt to move some of the green plume out of my face. Glorian looked back at me, a look of understanding in his eyes. We didn't give up when it got a little rough. He nodded.

"You can go if you want. I can distract it while you get to the door."

"And leave you here? You know, I've actually come to like you, Blaidd." He smiled weakly. Before I got the chance to respond, Uhhhhh made its way from the statue to where we were, spraying a bout of acid at the pillar. Glorian and I both bolted, side-by-side down the hall.

"Ah, but will you after this?" I grinned, not taking a glance at my friend as we turned a corner, sliding past the open door and behind another pillar.

"I think so. How big was the pay again?" He could barely get the words out without a laugh, and I found myself laughing as well, the two of us running for our lives, laughing in an underground deathtrap.

"I have an idea—" I looked at Glorian, pausing as I pressed my back against a pillar, gasping for breath after our short sprint. "But you're going to have to trust me." I looked around the pillar at the beast making its way towards us.

"Of course, captain."

I nodded with a smile, then sprinted out from the pillar to the center of the room, the beast turning away from where Glorian was behind the pillar, pursuing me with another scream.

"TO THE DOOR!" I screamed as loud as my lungs would let me, and saw Glorian following my instruction out of the corner of my eye. Uhhhhh swiped at me and spewed more acid at me almost at the same time, just barely dodging yet again.

I ran under the legs of the beast, my eyes on the doorway of the crystal-lined caves. Glorian was already inside as I slid in, the creature now making a move to follow me. Glorian and I both took several paces back, certain Uhhhhh would be too big to reach the inside of the doorway. I was proven wrong as the beast got closer, and it was realized that it in fact was the perfect size to fit into the door.

"I wondered—" I murmured.

"IT CAN CHANGE IT'S SIZE!?" My companion shrieked, and the two of us began running down the tunnel. We continued until reaching the stairs, where we bolted upwards, Uhhhhh screaming and clicking the whole way up.

I made sure Glorian stayed just in front of me as we made our way up the staircase. "GO GO

GO!" I barked, and that was all I could keep from pushing the elf up as the beast got closer behind me. Immediately once reaching the surface, I began to throw the biggest rocks I could find down, pieces of the wall that had broken off, doing what I could to block the tunnel.

"Do you really think that will stop it?" Glorian cried.

"No, but it will stall him, and that's enough." Glorian nodded at my words, and the two of us began to work together to lift a rather large piece of broken wall, pushing it down and over the tunnel entrance, letting it go with a loud SLAM!

The noise echoed through the night, and I was shocked to find myself jumping at the sound of a voice coming from several feet behind me. I reached immediately for my sword, before remembering it was currently inside the beast that was in the tunnel. Part of me hoped I was right that Uhhhhh would break through the stone. I liked that sword.

"What are you doing?" The voice of the brown-haired girl who I had fought earlier, Narissa, I reminded myself, came from up on a piece of the broken wall where she stood, sword in hand, pointed at Glorian and I. My companion pulled one of his throwing knives from his belt, holding it firmly in his hand.

"Oh, I just thought it would be fun to throw some rocks," I shrugged, sorting just as Uhhhhh let out another scream that caused the earth below to shake violently.

"WHAT WAS THAT!" Narissa screamed, jumping back down off the stone she was standing on.

"Uhhhhh." Glorian and I said in unison.

Part Twelve

Up in the Air (literally)

The beast broke through the stone with a loud crash, followed by an enraged scream. "I think we made it mad—" I murmured, casting a glance at Glorian, who nodded.

"You definitely made it mad," he mumbled, his knuckles whitening as he gripped the knife.

"Oh, blaming me, I see—"

"WHAT IS HAPPENING!!" Narissa screamed, sword in one hand, the other out with a glowing white mist—magic—flowing off her fingertips.

"Oh, Honeysuckle, meet Uhhhhh, Uhhhhhh, meet Honeysuckle," I bowed slightly to both the beast and the girl just before the creature let out another scream, and Glorian and I both bolted, the girl casting the magic on her hand onto her sword, making the steel of the blade glow white. She did not move, holding her ground. As the creature let out another scream, it sprayed acid in the girl's direction. I screamed for her to move, stopping my running to watch as the acid went around her, as the magic from her blade seemed to be casting some type of shield around her.

"Cool—" Glorian too had stopped running, the two of us watching as she lunged at the creature. Still, some distance away, she slammed her sword down, a cascade of magic slamming down on the beast. It screamed as if the blade had hit it, and I seized the opportunity to bolt at the creature, my knife still in hand. I ran straight up the beat, up its wing, and using the knife as a grip, jabbed it into the creature's side to pull myself up the rest of the way. I flung myself up, jumping over its second wing till I stood wobbly on top of the dragwyvdrawocky, digging my claws into the creature to keep myself from falling off.

The beast immediately began to trying to shake and throw me off, and the girl screamed something at me that I couldn't hear over the scream of the beast. As the creature thrashed around, I crouched, making my way to my sword. I reached my hand out, barely reaching the hilt as the beast spread its wings, thrusting itself into the air. I heard Glorian scream my name as the dragwyvdrawocky flew into the night sky. I crouched lower, both hands fixed to the wooden handle of my rapier, ears flat against my head.

A flash of white came from below, and it was easy enough to guess Narissa had used the magic of her sword again. I clenched my jaw as Uhhhhh lurched sharply to the side to avoid the burst of magic, letting out another scream as the magic managed to hit its leg. Instead of landing, Uhhhhh's four wings thrust harder, pushing us higher into the sky.

"I think that's high enough, buddy—" I lifted my hands to cover my ears as Uhhhhh let out the loudest and most aggressive scream yet, even my magic wasn't strong enough to shield myself from the ear-splitting pain the screech caused. The dragwyvdrawocky began to spray the acid below at Narissa and Glorian, and the best I could do was hope they were able to avoid it. Slowly and steadily, I lifted my weight, now conscious of the fact that Uhhhhh had seemed to decide this was high enough, bouncing slightly with each flap of his wings, but not getting any higher or lower in the air than he already was.

I pulled the sword from the creature's back, using my magic to null the sound and as much of the feeling of the blade's removal as I could, although my practice in healing magic was extremely limited. I was not surprised when the creature tried to throw me off again, this time I was prepared, grabbing onto one of the horns on its head as it did its best to shake me off as if I was some type of bug on the back of a dog.

One hand on my sword, the other on one of the beast's horns, I did the only logical thing and began to swing, kicking my legs back and forth to gain momentum as the creature continued to try its best to throw me off. My hand began to ache from the grip, and I began to question the logic of wearing all the rings I did (but really, who doesn't like to have shiny fingers?). I continued to swing, despite the creature practically spinning in mid-air to throw me off, and once I felt like I had enough, I thrust myself harder than before, curving my back and letting go of the horn, now freefalling in the face of the beast. I lifted my sword and slammed it down into Uhhhhhs skull, and with a scream, I knew it would not recover from the blow.

I wasted no time pushing my paws against the beast as we began to plummet, hoping with enough momentum I would be able to reach a nearby tree. I just barely managed to grab onto the branches, the thin limb immediately snapping as the impact of my sudden weight was a little too much. "I'm sorry!" I screamed to the tree as I fell through its branches, gasping as the wind was forced out of me and my back slammed hard against the ground. I closed my eyes, taking a moment to regain my senses—a bad ideas the reality of how much pain I was in began to set in.

I hadn't noticed at the moment, but as I was thrown around the creature, its sharp scales practically skinned my left arm, chest, and side, the horns from when I had been holding onto the creature cutting a nice deep cut along my face and neck, not to mention the wound to my leg from earlier, and the definitely broken bones from my fall.

Glorian ran over to me, the girl following. "Blaidd!" The moon elf screamed, crouching down beside me. I opened my eyes to meet with the silver eyes of the elf wich where beginning to water.

"Oh, calm down, I'm not dying—" I mused, a smile spreading on my face. I watched as he wiped his face with his arm, and I was unable to ignore the acid burns that traced along it. I clenched my jaw.

"You ok, kid?" I let my smile fall, and he nodded. I tilted my head as my eyes began to travel to the girl who was standing a small distance away from Glorian and me, her back against a tree.

"She is fine—" Glorian mumbled, his eyes flicking over to her. I nodded and pushed myself up, wincing, my arms immediately hugging my stomach, dropping my sword, and focused on the pain.

"We need to get the stone—" I spoke through my teeth, my hand reaching for my sword. Glorian nodded, his arm going around my body. The elf helped me up, and we began to fumble through the woods, Narissa following a few paces behind.

"Going back to your ship?" she asked conversationally as we walked. I smiled widely, looking back at her.

"Love, we came out here for a reason. You don't think we would give up after slaying the dragon, do you?" I was unable to stop from laughing, no matter how much it hurt my insides.

"We aren't just giving you the rock—not after doing all that." Glorian sounded as if he was ready to bite the brunette, which just made me laugh harder. "Blaidd, please stop laughing—you are scaring me." He mumbled just loud enough for me to hear.

I collapsed to my knees, hugging my stomach, laughing in pain. I felt like I was dying, the various injuries spread through my body giving me little hope of relief any time soon. Not that I thought I was going to die, but I sure felt like it. I stayed where I was, each breath of laughter shooting more pain through my body, but I also found myself unable to stop. If I stopped, I would begin to cry, and that, in front of others, was simply something I did not do.

Between the laughing and the ringing in my ears, I could barely hear Glorian as he screamed my name, not noticing the thick coating of red that was now soaking my body. I closed my eyes tightly, not that it would matter if my eyes were open, my vision so blurred and unfocused I couldn't make much sense of what I would see anyway.

I felt a hand on my back, and winced, my body shuttering at the pain the simple touch caused. In a moment, however, the hand remained where it was, and the pain steadily began to fade. My body realized that a cool wash of relief had steadily covered my body. My laughter slowly faded as the pain did, replaced with heavy breaths.

"Try to breathe normally," Narissa's voice was focused yet soft. What I now knew to be her hand was still on my back. I did as she instructed, albeit difficult.

"We need to get him to a proper healer."

"There isn't any on the ship and we are several days away from the nearest city!"

"He will die if we do not, the most I can do is numb the pain, not heal him."

I could just barely make out the conversation, my mind still trying to focus on my breaths, while also trying to ignore just how much it hurt still. I felt the hand remove itself from my back, moving to grab onto my chin, lifting it, forcing me to look up. When I opened my eyes, they were met with the brilliant brown eyes of Narissa.

"Hello, love," I smiled weakly. She did not find my comment amusing, rolling her eyes.

"If I didn't know of the people that rely on you, I would let you die. You do understand that, do you?"

"Understood," I grimaced. Narissa let go of my chin with another eye roll.

"The stone—" Glorian mumbled. Both Narissa and I looked at him, my eyes widening in realization as the brunette still seemed to be trying to understand the boy's meaning.

"For... anyone pure of heart—" he spoke slowly as if trying to remember what I had said about the glorified rock.

"It withholds the desired enchantment of the one who holds it," Narissa finished, nodding as she was now coming to the same conclusion Glorian had. She pushed herself to her feet in an instant, however, Glorian too rose, knife in hand.

"How do we know you aren't just going to take it and run?"

"I guess you're just going to have to trust me."

"You've made that easy," Glorian said sarcastically.

"Listen, I could have run for it the second the beast was killed. Trust me or not, he is going to die without my help. I am going with or without your blessing, and I suggest you give it before I do decide to take the stone and run!" Narissa practically screamed at Glorian, her hands moving to emphasize her words as she spoke. When she went silent, she stared into Glorian, glaring.

"Okay," the elf spoke after a long moment of silence.

"I trust you," I finally spoke, pushing myself up against a tree, a weak smile on my face, eyes on Narissa. She looked back at me for some time through the night, the wind softly blowing her hair, the light from the moons and stars just enough to see through the darkness. She nodded, and within a moment, ran into the forest.

Part Thirteen

Air Pure of heart

Darting as fast as her legs could take her, Narissa bolted through the forest, not caring as branches hit her, scratched her, and tore her garments. She didn't know why she felt like she needed to save the mercenary, but something inside her told her she had to, beyond simple compassion. Her pace did not slow as she moved around the dead beast that lay on the ground, simply avoiding the creature and heading straight towards the tunnel, where she made her way inside.

Narissa didn't let herself get distracted by the now damaged and broken crystals that lined the cave tunnel, only slowing her pace so as not to trip on the debris that lay on the cave ground. When the creature had traveled through the tunnel, it hadn't had any type of care, making quite a mess of the cave as it had plowed its way through.

Now becoming weary, Narissa paused in front of the broken door that led to the main cavern, taking slow steps inside the moonlit room. Her hand lowered, resting on the hilt of her blade, ready to pull it at a moment's notice if need be. The stillness was almost off-putting after the fight that had just happened. Narissa wasn't used to stillness, and the idea made her weary. After a few more steps, however, she came to the realization that she had no need to be wary. The room was empty, apart from the large stature of a girl before her.

"You're holding it, aren't you?" the brunette sighed, lifting her hand from her sword, walking up to the statue until she was mere feet away, her head up to look at the angelic figure that towered above her. "Why was the beast in here... did it find its way and saw this as an ideal nest... or did you put it here?

Narissa surveyed the statue for some time, unsure where the stone would be. She had to climb the statue to fully check, but something about that notion seemed disrespectful somehow. While she wasn't sure, the four wings and halos gave the brunette a pretty good idea of whom the statue was to represent, and if she was right, well, she, for one, did believe in the Divine guardians of Eritis, and their creator.

"Is there a magic word—or like a password—that you'll just give it to me?" Her thoughts were interrupted as she spotted the glimmer of light that reflected on the statue, where the two halos intersected just above the girl's forehead sat A small diamond-shaped crystal.

Without hesitation, Narissa began to climb the statue, pushing herself up and maneuvering around the statue until her legs perched on the arms, reaching for the stone. Her hand grazed the stone, Narissa quickly realizing it wasn't going to simply pop out of the statue. She reached for the knife strapped to her thigh and carefully used it to pry the stone from the statue.

Once it was out, she took a moment of pause to survey the crystal. The Harbinger Stone was smaller than Narissa had been expecting, only a few centimeters, truly only big enough for a ring or small pendant. It was clear, and yet it withheld every color imaginable, with a light outshining any diamond, enchanted or not. It seemed to glow from within as if a fallen star had been trapped within its depths. Its brilliance was so intense that it cast a soft, ethereal glow on everything around it. The magic it radiated was extraordinary, a blend of peace and raw power that Narissa had never felt before. It was a unique force, blessed by Grace herself, and it filled the girl with a sense of tranquility and awe. As Narissa gazed into its depths, she felt a connection to something ancient and powerful, truly unlike anything else.

"Sorry, m'lady," the brunette spoke as she pocketed the stone, made her way down the statue, and ran out of the room.

"I got it!" Narissa came running towards Glorian and I, and while a small part of me had begun to wonder if she would be coming back, I couldn't help but smile knowing she had done just that. In the time the brunette had been gone, Glorian had done his best to tend to my wounds, but with little to no supplies on either of us, it made it a little more than difficult.

Narissa crouched beside me, pulling the small stone from her pocket and holding it loosely in her hand. She closed her eyes, expecting the magic to be enacted, but nothing happened. Glorian looked at her in confusion.

"You aren't going to do it, are you? Not going to use your enchantment?"

"N-no, I'm trying—" she opened her eyes, brow furrowed in fear and confusion as she loosened her hand, eyes on the stone that glittered in the moonlight.

"I guess it decided you aren't pure of heart," I spoke quietly about what everyone was thinking, and we made eye contact. Narissa clenched her jaw, knowing I was right. I slowly held out my hand, and she dropped it in my pawm.

I looked at the stone, willing for the healing of my wounds, pushing my mind to think of only positive things. After a moment, however, I began to laugh. "I can't use it." I winced at my own laughter, the pain had slowly been coming back to my body in the twenty or so minutes Narissa had been gone, so the simple action made my head spin.

"Let's be honest, none of us thought I—" I started but was quickly interrupted by Glorian.

"Maybe it's because you're trying to use it on yourself? Would that count as selfish?"

"Do I look Grace-standard pure of heart to you?" I mused, realizing for the first time that I might actually die from my wounds. If I had gotten aid earlier, I may not have, but the bleeding wasn't stopping, and with nothing to close the wounds, I was most certainly going to bleed out.

"No," Glorian mumbled. "I don't believe that." He clenched his jaw, the star like freckles on his skin glowing in the moonlight. He showed no sign of tears, only a look of genuine determination. The elf placed his hand over mine, his silver eyes beginning to match the glow of the crystal in my hand. I smiled, my ears falling back slightly. Our eyes met, his eyes wide.

"Yeah, that makes sense," I laughed lightly. Narissa stood back, her eyes focused on Glorian. Once realizing he was able to use the stone, he closed his eyes, telling the stone of his desired enchantment. A wash of magic covered my body, focusing around me. The pain left my body almost immediately as the magic came in contact with my flesh, all wounds healing. While I was still covered in blood, where open wounds stood before, were only scars.

Once the magic faded and the light dimmed, Glorian opened his eyes, laughing slightly upon noting the healed wounds, leaning and hugging onto me.

"Thanks, kid," I smiled when he pulled away, the elf quickly wiping his now teary eyes.

"Im only a year younger."

"But im still older."

The two of us began to laugh, only looking up as Narissa stood with a nod as if she had decided something. I looked up to her, Glorian's eyes darting between the two of us as he straightened himself.

"You're leaving?" Even as I spoke it, I knew it wasn't really a question. Narissa had made up her mind.

"I don't know what you need the Harbinger Stone for, but I trust you with it," she said, her direction changing from me to Glorian.

"I am still very unsure about you," she glared at me, but her lips lifted to a smile, then a nod. With that, she began to walk into the forest. Both Glorian and I pushed ourselves to our feet, watching the girl leave. After a few steps, however, I couldn't help myself as I felt the stone in my hand.

"What were you going to use it for?" I asked, causing Narissa to pause.

"It doesn't matter now, does it?" She turned her head back to us, eyes on me.

"Maybe it does." I felt the stone in my hand, turning the warm surface over in my fingers. I could barely believe what I was thinking of doing, insane really, and how mad would the King of Shadows be if I failed?

"I don't want it." Narissa remarked, a smile still on her face.

"How about passage wherever you are heading on my ship? It's the least I can offer after—"

"I appreciate the offer, but quite frankly, I'm not a fan of Wolves." she spoke with amusement in her tone, a sound I found to be a lovely thing. "That's not your real name, is it?"

"No," I laughed, "it's not."

Part Thirteen

The King of Shadows' proposal (not that kind, ya weirdo)

I pulled the Harbinger Stone from my pocket, turning it over in my hands for a moment, my eyes fixed on it. A sigh left my lips as I looked up into the piercing white eyes of Mogotsi, standing over me, then dropped the stone into his large hand. In silence, the two of us made eye contact, and I felt as if he was staring into my soul. I wouldn't doubt it, knowing how powerful the guy was. The stone gleamed with a bright white light, which then faded out of view as the King of Shadows' large clawed fingers wrapped around the stone, then set it down on the table of the desk he now sat at.

"Your payment will be provided shortly. Thank you, your service is greatly appreciated, Romulus Neverglade."

"Not my name—" I mumbled, but was careful not to speak too loudly, not that I thought he couldn't hear me regardless. "Thanks," my tail swayed as the two of us now sat somewhat awkwardly. I had half the heart to walk away—hey, thanks Mr. Creepy Demon Shadow King guy for the money, see you never; hopefully—but something held me back, maybe it was curiosity or the hunch that he had more to say to me. After another moment of Mogotsi's eyes on me, I was proven to be right.

"You are certainly an interesting creature," he spoke, eyes not leaving contact with my own.

"Why, thank you!" I grinned, bowing. I felt Mogotsi Nightshade's mood lift in that very uncomfortable sense of sharing emotions thing he did, and was happy that it seemed he was amused. That was always a good sign.

"And you had no compulsion to keep the stone for yourself? Surely you understand with its ability, it could have been a great tool to you."

"Oh, it doesn't work for me," I laughed, straightening myself with a nod. Something in his mood shifted, but now I had no way to sense what it was exactly he was feeling. The only conclusion I could come to was a mix of emotions, or maybe he didn't even know what he was feeling.

"Truly..." His eyes were still on me—seriously, this guy's negative eyes were really hard to make contact with, and even more scary to just have staring at you.

"Yep," I nodded. "So is that all because—"

"It's not."

"Oh. Okay then."I began to play with one of the braids in my hair, waiting for him to speak. "I have a proposal for you."

"Wow, that was fast, not that you aren't my type and all, but at least like buy me—" We made eye contact.

"..."

"Sorry—"

"You greatly intrigue me, and I see potential in you... you will do something great one day—whether that be something good or bad, I do not know, however, I see our stories are to be intertwined from this point foreward."

"Gross," I was unable to stop myself—my mind was racing—great things? Me? Yeah, not going to happen. The thought didn't even make me smile, and the knowledge that this greatness could be a bad thing wasn't exactly something that excited me. Heck, gosh darn it, I was scared. "Sorry—"

"Do you wish to hear what I have to say? If not, I will not waste your time." He spoke as I lowered my head. After a moment of thought, I nodded.

"I sense that neither of us desires for your greatness to be a bad thing, and because of this, I would like to offer you a place under me, as an apprentice, to word it simply."

"What—" I laughed slightly. I knew Mr. King wasn't exactly the joking type, but well, keeping my mouth shut was never something I was exactly good at. "I'm a mercenary," I mused, my words lined with confusion. I was unable to keep my ears from lowering despite this, a mix of anger and emotion I wasn't quite expecting.

"I have a crew to take care of, and jobs to fulfill, and I can't just abandon them to come train under you?! I understand you are a great and powerful mage and everything, but I—" I had barely noticed as my hand lowered to the hilt of my blade—a practiced move, feeling the metal-lined wood in my hand, then slowly lowered it.

"Why would you want to train me of all people?" I couldn't even force the mock humor I usually carried, my words low as I tried to keep the emotion out of my voice. No one had ever offered to take me under their wing. Everything I had ever done, I had been the one to ask, or follow, or beg—a place to stay, a job, even when I had been in Faerie, while I was taken in, so to speak, I had been the one to ask to stay. I was not initially invited. It was why I had been so determined to always be the one to find people like myself and invite them to my crew. I didn't want them to go through what I had.

"As I explained, I see a great potential within you, and if you will allow it, I would take great pleasure in being the one to teach you."

"I—I don't know—"

"I do not require an answer now, take some time to think it over, to talk it over with your crew. Do not think I have forgotten, or discounted them from my offer. It extends to them as well. Not to take them under me personally, of course, but they may stay at my castle, everything they will need will be provided for them, and you may make this your home port if you so desire. Much as I required your services for the stone, there are other tasks that I have need of assistance, so if you and your crew desire, you may serve under me, and have my protection. I am happy to give you any and all details you desire regarding the entire apprenticeship and situation.”

I had to admit it was a good offer, and despite the fact that we were used to our nomadic lifestyle, to have a home port and to be able to live off the ship for a while was something I knew not just myself craved.

“How do I know I can trust you?” Even as I spoke, the memory of the glowing crystal in his hand flashed before my mind, that in itself telling me he had no ill intent.

“That is yours for you to decide, as I know mere words can mean nothing. If it is any consolation, you would not be the first for me to train, and in fact, even now you would have another alongside you in many of your lessons.”

“Oh?” I prompted, unsure how I felt about that.

"Her lessons are all but complete, and as of now, she is more of a courtier of mine, but I feel you may find her company favorable."

"Her...?"

As if on cue, the sound of footsteps echoed through the halls of the large building, leading to the office Mogotsi and I were sitting in. The door pushed open, revealing a cloaked woman. "I'm sorry to intrude, but—" As she spoke, I couldn't help but recognize the voice, a wide grin spreading over my face as Narissa threw down the hood of her cloak, letting her hair fall down onto her shoulders.

"YOU?" I tensed, turning to her, hand on my sword. She did the same.

"YOU!" She snapped. "What are you doing here?! Master, he—" Her muscles relaxed upon seeing the relaxed state that Mogotsi was in, and it didn't take me long to figure out what exactly was happening.

"I hired him to get the stone, much as I sent you," Mogotsi's eyes trailed to Narissa, who started back in absolute confusion.

"THIS is the new apprentice you were talking about?!" she breathed incredulously. My eyes trailed between the two. He had been watching me, and had been planning to offer me an apprenticeship since I gathered the stone for him—an interesting notion that made me even more unsure if I should accept or not.

"It is."

"Why send both of us?!" the brunette snapped, her hands stretched out to express her words as she had done before when we had interacted. Kind of cute.

"He wanted to see who would win," I mumbled, eyes again trailing from Narissa to Mogotsi. The King of Shadows placed his hand back to the small stone, tapping it with his pointer finger.

"It was a test for both of you. I desired to see if the two of you would work together, and to see how you would interact. If you would make a good team," he lifted his eyes, his attention more on Narissa than myself. She lowered her head, clearly thinking the same thing I had. We had fought, tried to kill each other, even, before taking the time to understand each other's needs, not caring for a split second what the other one of us needed with the Harbinger Stone, or why we were searching for it. The only time either of us showed any care for the other was when Narissa had gone to get the stone to help me, and even let me take the stone, with the knowledge of Mogotsi in wait for it. In that, I saw she was a much better person than myself.

"Why did you let me take it?" My eyes fixed on Narissa, who crossed her arms. Mogotsi tilted his head, and despite his lack of emotions, I could tell he was starting to wonder about our interaction.

"While, of course, Mogotsi has need of it—I—" She looked at me as she spoke, her brown eyes struggling to keep contact with mine. "I thought you needed it more," she finally admitted, looking away from me when she was done speaking. From the corner of my eye, I saw Mogotsi nod.

"I will leave the two of you then. I only came to say that I had not retrieved the stone, but I can see you already know." Narissa eyed the stone on the desk, then nodded to the gargoyle.

"Narissa—" I started before she got the chance to leave the room. The way the girl looked at me made me think she was about to attack me, but after a moment, her brow raised in anticipation. "Thank you," I smiled a genuine smile, nodding to her in a half bow. The brunette nodded to me in what I imagined was her way of saying you're welcome, and left the room.

"Don't get mad at her for not getting the stone," I turned back to Mogotsi, my gaze focused on him.

"She did exactly as I anticipated she would do. There is nothing for me to be mad about." I could tell he was being honest, which prompted a nod from me.

"Now, Blaidd Delphire, regarding my proposal..."

Acknowledgments

If you made it all the way to the end! Oh my gosh, thank you so much for reading Book One of the Delphire series! I hope you enjoyed it, and if you did, I promise there is more to come in this tale—a lot more.

I have been working on this story in the back of my head for YEARS. It's been an Instagram novel, a webtoon, a series of ballads (I said what I meant), a novel, and FINALLY, I got to where I am now with a light novel series!

This story and Romulus/Blaidd himself as a character is a representation of myself in a lot of ways, so finally stepping out and sharing his story has been something I have both been extremely excited and absolutely horrified to do. I want to thank all of my friends who have been there for and with me along the way, through my life, and while I've worked on this story. Rip my attempts to keep it a secret. I could go on for hours explaining all the things my best friends have done for me, but I will try to keep it short.

Dear my favorite people in the whole wide world (literally none of us better have a friend breakup or this would get really awkward):

Mia, who owns Blaidd's family: It's obvious why I have to mention you first. Thank you so much for being my friend over the years, for the talks and the laughs, the tears, and all of the crazy stuff we have done since we met when we were little. You are such an amazing light and truly an inspiration in my life, and one of my best friends. I love you, girl.

Kat: Not only the best cousin one could ask for, you are literally awesome. You have helped me through so much in my life, you can't even begin to understand what you have done for me without even knowing. I see you as more of a sister than a cousin, but I guess getting to flaunt that we are already blood is good enough. I love you dearly, keep being yourself, and don't ever let life get in the way of that.

Megan: Oh my gosh, girl, don't get me started. I may not have known you for quite as long, but you became such an amazing friend to me so quickly. The little things you do, and your sweet and genuine heart is just amazing. I didn't know they made people as genuine as you are anymore, but I see I've been proven wrong. You have helped me through so much through simple acts, and honestly, become one of my best friends quicker than I could ever have imagined.

Sam: Don't think I forgot you. This whole book is dedicated to you after all. Sometimes I can't understand how we are still friends after all these years, after all the problems I have caused. I literally love you so much. You have done so much for me and been with me through so many things, good and bad. I can't begin to thank you for everything, but I hope this is enough to get the point across. I love you, mate.

I don't want to bore you with a lot of talk, so I'll leave it there for now. Hope to see you at Book Two!

Have Random Character sheets

Glorian Autumnbrush
He/Him / 5'8 / Moonelf

Narissa Thayer
She/Her /5,4 / halfelf